CHRISTMAS IN
MY SOUL

CHRISTMAS IN MY SOUL

A Third Collection

Compiled and Edited by

JOE WHEELER

Doubleday

New York London Toronto Sydney Auckland

PUBLISHED BY DOUBLEDAY
a division of Random House, Inc.
1540 Broadway, New York, NY 10036

DOUBLEDAY and the portrayal of an anchor with a
dolphin are registered trademarks of Doubleday,
a division of Random House, Inc.

Book design by Dana Leigh Treglia

Woodcut illustrations from the library of Joe Wheeler

Cataloging-in-publication data is on file with the
Library of Congress.

ISBN 0-385-49861-6

PRINTED IN THE UNITED STATES OF AMERICA

November 2002
First Edition

1   3   5   7   9   10   8   6   4   2

A number of years ago, a friendly voice came into my life, a voice with a smile attached. In fact, I can't ever remember a time when his voice failed to radiate happiness. Along the way, he has become a treasured friend. Thus it gives me great pleasure to dedicate this collection of stories to my Doubleday editor.

ANDREW CORBIN

Acknowledgments

Introduction: "Home for Christmas," by Joe Wheeler. Copyright © 2000 (revised 2001). Printed by permission of the author.

"When Tad Remembered," by Minnie Leona Upton. Published in *The Youth's Instructor*, December 22, 1925. Reprinted by permission of Joe Wheeler (P.O. Box 1246, Conifer, CO 80433) and Review and Herald Publishing Association, Hagerstown, Md.

"The Stuffed Kitten," by Mae Hurley Ashworth. Published in *The Town Journal*, December 1953. If anyone can provide knowledge of the origin and first publication source of this story, please relay this information to Joe Wheeler, care of Doubleday Religion Department.

Contents

CHRISTMAS IN

MY SOUL

INTRODUCTION

....

Home for Christmas

Joseph Leininger Wheeler

ome for Christmas"—are there three sweeter words in the English language? After all, taken singly, "home" and "Christmas" are two of the most loaded-with-sentiment words we know; together, their freight is almost mind-boggling. But leaving aside the rich connotative dimensions of these two words, let's start with laying our discussional foundation on bedrock—the dictionary definitions of our two key words: "home" and "Christmas," for it is surprising how often the obvious escapes us.

HOME: n. 1. A place where one lives; residence; habitation. 2. The physical structure or portion thereof within which one lives, as a house or apartment. 3. One's close family and one's self, a person's most personal relationships and posses- sions; *house and home.* 4. An environment or haven of shelter, of happiness and love. 5. Any valued place, original habitation, or emotional at- tachment regarded as a refuge or place of origin. 6. The place where one was born or spent his early childhood, as a town, state, or country. 7. The native habitat of a plant, animal, or the like. 8. The place where something is discovered, founded, developed, or promoted. 9. A headquar- ters or base of operations from which activities are coordinated; home base.

The American Heritage Dictionary of
the English Language
(Boston: Houghton Mifflin Company, 1976)

CHRISTMAS: 1. December 25, a holiday cele- brated by Christians as the anniversary of the birth of Jesus. 2. The Christian church festival extending from December 24 (Christmas Eve) through

January 6 (Epiphany). In this sense, also called "Christmastide."

American Heritage Dictionary

So, first of all, a "home" is a definite place: region, town, piece of land, house. We all conceptualize in concrete terms, consequently when we think of going home, we visualize it first as a part of the country; next as a town or place; then as a farm, ranch, or piece of ground; and finally as a building. It is because of this sequential perception of home that the first wave of homecoming joy washes over us when we enter the region of home: Whatever it may be, mountains, rolling hills, plains, desert, or seacoast, the effect is the same. Speaking for myself, since I was born only a few miles from the coast of California, driving west, once the car crests the Sierra Nevadas and starts down toward the San Joaquin Valley, I sense I'm nearing home; but when my senses tell me the ocean is near—even before I can see it—a much bigger wave of joy floods me; and oh that first vision of the Pacific! It almost stops my heart in its tracks. Since there is no ancestral home still in family hands, and I cannot bear to seek out my grandparents' Napa Valley Shangrila high on Howell Mountain, for fear of what I'd find after the long years (perhaps it is now demolished completely), I'd rather dream that it still exists as I once knew and loved it. Because of this, it is the ocean that represents "home" to me. But had I been born in the mountains, as I was in a sense in the Napa Valley region, that too is home. Same for those born on the Great Plains—to them, mountains are claustrophobic; and to those born and raised on the desert, no other terrain can ever be as beautiful as the sunburned and windswept sage.

Some blessed few are fortunate enough to be born, raised, and do their growing up in one locale, one house, and be able to return to it late in life and find it intact and in the family still—but few of us in this hurried and dysfunctional age are that lucky. Some months ago, my sister Marjorie and I took my mother to Chico, California, where Mom had lived for a time in her earliest childhood. We found the street easy enough but a number of the landmarks my mother remembered were no longer there. Finally we narrowed it down to a two-block area, then one—then we found it! Fortunately, Chico has preserved that street as a historic district. We went in and found out it is a doctor's office now, but amazingly the place had seen very little remodeling in eighty years. My mother was very quiet as she looked on, and quiet afterward, so I really don't know what kind of an impact the experience had on her, but I know how my sister and I responded: There, in this lovely old home, surrounded by towering trees, is a piece of Mother's life—she showed us the bedroom that was hers and the window through which she viewed her childhood world.

As for my own childhood, being the child of teachers, a minister father, missionary parents, I have no one childhood place to consider home. That's why the homes of my paternal and maternal grandparents mean so much to me; for no matter where my parents moved, those two houses remained a constant. Thus they each represented four walls we could depend upon. Without such symbols of stability, children feel lost. Readers may remember my paternal grandparents' Napa Valley home in "Legacy," a Christmas story I wrote some years ago, but I had another home to come home to, as well: that great rambling two-story house in Arcata, California, belonging to Grandma and Grandpa Leininger. I lived with them my eighth grade year, and that year represents one of the most happy and loved periods of my lifetime, and is woven into the very fiber of my being. In those far-off days before so much logging had taken place, Arcata was one of the foggiest places on the planet, very conducive to the acres of fuchsia, asters, and so on, that Grandpa grew for his florist business; behind the house was a towering redwood forest that seemed to my childish eyes to stretch away forever, complete with trilliums, ferns, and a magical lake that I considered my own possession. Across Highway 101 we could hear the sounds of the lumber mill, night and day. At night, I'd look out my attic window at the ghostly headlights, heading I knew not where on the highway—and I'd dream of the people inside, and wonder about their destinations (readers may remember that house in my earlier Christmas story "The Third Rose"). It was listening to my grandfather recite Shakespeare and Kipling by the hour—what an actor he would have made!—and seeing him transposing the news of the day on walls of *National Geographic* maps that helped to set my personal sails for life: decide to major in English and history. I submit, in this respect, that children who never get to spend extended time with their grandparents (preferably without those authority figures—parents—around) miss out on a large piece of their selfhood and family heritage.

Since my parents moved so often, when I conceptualize "home" in my mind, I telescope a number of houses in a number of countries, each of which was "home" for a time. What counted was my parents' love for each other: *That* was the real essence of the term to us. As long as that remained constant, moving from one set of four walls to another was merely another adventure. When a move had been completed, and the furniture and possessions had been reassembled in the old way, we children were just as much "home" as before the move took place.

Which brings us to the sad reality of a divorce-ridden society. In my lifetime of research and reading, dealing with students of all ages, including adults twenty-two to eighty in an Adult Degree Program I directed, I am convinced beyond a shadow of a doubt that a child *never* fully recovers from separation or divorce. Whether the remembering interval encompasses six months or sixty years, the result is the same. Over and over and over again, I have heard their life stories, and when they come to that period of separation, they slow their telling or reading, they begin to choke up, tears begin to flow, and often the story grinds to a complete halt—the group is forced to leave for a while, reassemble, and hope the man or woman will find it possible to continue. That act of desertion creates a chasm in the child's psyche, a gulf ever after separating the world that was from the world that came after—*never* does that chasm close, even when the parents remarry: The terrible damage to the child's sense of selfhood, self-worth, and belonging cannot be undone, no matter how many years may pass. Up till the act of separation, the child may realize that there are cracks in "home," but the walls are still standing; that is very different from a collapse of the entire structure.

A tragic by-product of the disintegration of the marriage for life as we once knew it is the soaring suicide rate during the Christmas season. We can hide our brokenness from others most of the time, but at Christmas we cannot hide it even from ourselves.

I have never doubted my selfhood or my gifts, because there were no perceived cracks in the home I grew up in; the same is not true of children of divorce I have interacted with through the years: Every last one of them has seen something tragic happen to that protective wall, that fortress each of us needs as a bastion to retreat into during the struggles of life. Each always questions those walls, retreats to them but not as to an inviolate sanctuary. As long as they live, they must be reassured continually in terms of their self-worth. The pain is assuaged and, over the years, even heals, but the effects—never.

So it is that when a child of separation or divorce thinks of "home" at Christmastime, it will be in a different way than I do—even when the parents remarry and the stepparents are kind and loving to them. "Home" to them may very well be a fragmentation between four or more sets of steprelationships, thus no one of them is perceived wholistically. But this does not mean that a home with a stepparent may not be seen as the closest and dearest "home" that child could imagine, for some blessed stepparents bring to that later "home" all the qualities that were missing in the first.

But, having said all this, when the subject comes up as to whether or not to go, or not go, home for Christmas, other variables come into play, chief of which is this: Are the rewards of "going home" worth the expenditure of effort and money? If bickering is likely, the answer is likely to be no. If all anyone does there is watch TV, that could be done just as easily and much cheaper by staying put. No, those who will joyfully invest effort, time, and money in "going home for Christmas" do so because going there is likely to be such joy that it would be unthinkable not to be there to be part of it.

Going home also brings home to each of us a great truth: We are all getting older—the children become adolescents, the adolescents become teenagers, the teenagers become young adults, the young adults become young marrieds, the young marrieds become middle-aged, the middle-aged become senior citizens, and the senior citizens become debilitated and lose their mental and physical edge, and then are taken from the family's holiday festivities by death. In truth, such family reunions represent a way of measuring the passing of time, thus we do indeed measure our lives by our Christmases. Bitter though it is to see those we love most weakening under the battering of the years, that sight does make us love and cherish them the more, recognizing that the time may not be afar off when we will no longer have that privilege. Furthermore, when that sad day *does* come at last, we will still have all the wondrous memories to replay each Christmas: "Remember the time when—," and it is as though that dearly beloved person is part of the circle still.

Interestingly enough, as everything goes in cycles, today, even the children of divorce are seeking a stability and sense of bedrock they never knew. Traditions are coming back again, as are other "old-fashioned" things such as integrity, decency, loyalty, faithfulness, kindness, empathy, generosity, altruism, dependability, selflessness, and so forth. In the words of the musical *Carousel*, we as a society had "gone about as far as we could go" in the opposite direction of these qualities. Of course, always, at turn-of-centuries, each society totally reevaluates all the qualities by which it lives, and millennial-turns are even more seismic. So it is that, all across the nation, there is developing a new emphasis on values, family, and traditions that enrich life. Not surprisingly, there is renewed interest in making holidays such as Christmas not only more enjoyable but also more meaningful.

But going home for Christmas presupposes the existence of something else, and that is (1) the stability that comes with God-sanctified marriage as opposed to live-in relationships, (2) children—how true it is that none of us really grows up and becomes truly unselfish until we have our first child, (3) a family that has stayed together through the years (almost impossible to achieve without the help of a Higher Power), (4) the inclusion of the extended family (cousins, uncles, aunts, grandparents) into the celebration.

Our son Greg I call our "Christmas Boy," for ever

since he left home for the career world, no sooner is one Christmas celebration over than he wants to know where the next one is going to be held so he can plan ahead for it. I would guess that same love for this most special of seasons can be found everywhere where Christmas is celebrated as it should be (keeping in mind Whose birthday we are celebrating).

I too have always looked forward to "going home for Christmas." May the good Lord bless and guide you and yours as you too travel *home* for Christmas.

ABOUT THIS COLLECTION

While this is the third yearly *Christmas in My Soul* collection, it is the seventh annual collection by Doubleday, the first four being titled *Christmas in My Heart*. Thus new readers will wish to pick up copies of the earlier collections. Of the six authors presented in this collection, our readers will already be familiar with Temple Bailey ("The Candle in the Forest," "The Locking in of Lisabeth," "And It Was Christmas Morning," in the first, third, and fourth *Christmas in My Heart* treasuries). The others are new to this series.

CODA

Virtually every day's mail brings welcome correspondence from you. Many of your letters are testimonials to the power of certain stories; virtually *all* of them express gratitude for the series. Others include favorite stories for possible inclusion down the line (some of them Christmas-related and others tying in with other genre collections we are working on). These letters from you not only brighten each day for us but help to provide the stories that make possible future anthologies.

May the good Lord bless and guide each of you.

You may contact me at the following address:
Joe L. Wheeler, Ph.D.
c/o Doubleday Religion Department
1540 Broadway
New York, New York 10036

WHEN TAD REMEMBERED

....

Minnie Leona Upton

Mary Merivale turned, peered eagerly down the length of the quiet elm-shaded street; then the expectant light faded from her tired eyes. She had done this a full five thousand times—but still no Bobbie.

That was bad enough, but where was Taddy— Taddy, her beloved dog?

This story dates back about a hundred years ago, to a time when diseases such as diphtheria, typhoid, scarlet fever, cholera, tuberculosis, influenza, and so on, *came—there being no known antidotes—they wiped out entire families; when you add in death because of childbirth complications, you were lucky if half your children survived to adulthood. It was a mighty tough and heartbreaking time in which to live.*

This is an old story, and I have loved it ever since I first heard it, growing up. I have never been able to find anything about the author. In fact, this is the only one of her stories I have ever found. What a pity!

....

I t was closing time for a little notion shop that shyly besought the scant patronage of a sleepy, shabby old side street in a great city. The little notion shop lady sped a last lingering patron with a cheery but decided good-night, then following her outside, closed the snow-burdened blinds with tremulous haste, and, turning, peered eagerly down the length of the quiet, elm-shaded street. One long look, then the patient eyes from which the expectant light had suddenly faded turned for a moment to the remote keen December stars, and a tired little sigh accompanied the clicking of the key in the lock.

Full five thousand times had Mary Merivale done this, and nothing more interesting than Sandy Macpherson the cobbler, putting up his shutters, or old Bettina the apple woman, ambling homeward with empty basket, had yet rewarded her searching gaze. But it was part of her day, of her life: and the warm thrill of unreasoning hope had never failed to come. Next time—who could tell? Especially at Christmastime!

She hung the key on its nail, and limped back into her low-ceiled sitting room, dining room, kitchen. With resolute cheerfulness she opened the drafts, and woke the slumbering fire in the shining stove, lighted the rose-shaded lamp, drew the curtains, and filled the diminutive teakettle. She was beginning to spread a white cloth on the wee round table (having removed the Dresden shepherdess, and the pot of pansies, and the crocheted doily, and the cretonne cover), when her operations were interrupted by a vigorous scratching on the door opening into the backyard.

The little lady's face broke into a welcoming smile, deepening a host of pleasant wrinkles. She drew the bolt, the door burst open, and in bounded a little rough-coated, brownish-yellow—or yellowish-brown—mongrel, yapping joyously, and springing up, albeit somewhat laboriously and rheumatically, to bestow exuberant kisses upon the beloved hands of his lady.

"There, there, Taddy—there, there—that'll do," she said.

But there was not a marked firmness in the prohibition, and it was several minutes before Tad subsided, and sank, with asthmatic wheezes, upon a braided rug that looked as if it might have been made from Joseph's coat of many colors.

"Been watchin' for the rat, Taddy?"

Tad thumped the mat with his happy, lowbred, undocked tail. He took no shame to himself that a year's efforts had failed to catch and bring to justice the canny old rat that, under the wastebarrel house, made carefree entrances and exits through a hole that led to regions unknown. He knew nothing of the countless times when the bold bandit had skipped nonchalantly forth while he was taking forty winks.

Once the villain would not have escaped him so arrogantly, nor, indeed, at all! But almost twenty conscientiously active years, with asthma and rheumatism, had stolen away, bit by bit, his alertness of observation and elasticity of muscle, though not one iota of his warmth of heart and lightness of spirit.

He curled up contentedly on his rug, and watched proceedings with eager interest, now and then putting out an affectionately arresting paw when his mistress whisked near him in her bustling to and fro.

Presently his bowl of broth was set down before him, on a square of blue-and-white oilcloth, and his lady sat herself down to her frugal meal. It ended with a tiny square of fruitcake (brought in by an old customer) for the lady, and a lump of moist brown sugar for the dog.

"If you'd only chew it, Tad, 'pears to me you'd sense it more," observed Tad's mistress, in a tone of gentle reproach.

Tad promptly assumed an expression of penitence and hopefulness, fetchingly blended: not from any reason of the nature of his offense, but because that tone in her voice always indicated that he had done something; hopefulness, because of expectation of a small supplementary lump which he had hitherto received—he seeing no reason this night why the second lump should not continue. But tonight—tonight—no second lump was forthcoming.

The little woman spoke apologetically, "Tomorrow, I hope, Taddy dear, perhaps three lumps—who knows—business hasn't been very good this week [she had sold just seven cents' worth of notions, and the rent was due], and I never ask for it, you know."

Tad didn't know. But he felt the lump in the dear voice. He got up, stiffly, and laid his common little head in her lap, and looked comforting volumes with his great shining eyes. He licked the queer salty water that dropped on her hand from somewhere, and she began to smile, and call him her comfort, whereat he wagged hilariously.

Presently Mrs. Maguire, who had moved in next door, and whose red, white, and blue sign read, WASHING AND SCRUBBING DUN INSIDE OR OUT, ran in for a friendly chat. Neighborliness burgeons at Christmastime!

"A foine loively little dawg, Mis' Merivale!" she commented enthusiastically, directing an approving pat at Tad's rough head. It descended on air. Tad had flopped over on one side and was lying with one paw raised appealingly, one eye alertly open and the other tightly closed.

"Was ivver the loikes av thot, now, for the way of a dawg!" exclaimed the admiring Mrs. Maguire.

But Mary Merivale had dropped on her knees beside the little performer, tears and smiles playing hide-and-seek among her wrinkles.

"It's a trick my Bobbie taught 'im, when he was yet a wee-bit puppy near twenty years ago. Who's Bobbie? Why—but there, you're a newcomer in the neighborhood. Bobbie is my little boy—that is, he *was* my little boy. I—Mis' Maguire, there's something about you makes me feel you'd understand; somehow my heart and my head have been full of remembering today. I—I would so like to tell you about Bobbie, and how it is that I'm alone—if it wouldn't tire you—after your hard day's work."

"Mis' Merivale, just lit it pourr right out! It'll do the hearts of the two ov us good—you to pourr it out, an' me to take it in! I brought me Moike's sweater to darrn, an' its a good listenin' job."

A big red hand gave the soft gray waves of Mary Merivale's hair a gentle pat; then Mrs. Maguire began to rock to and fro as she threaded a huge darning needle and essayed to fill in a ragged aperture.

Mary Merivale, knitting swiftly on a sturdy red mitten, took up her story.

"Nineteen years ago last October, my husband died; the kindest, best husband that ever lived. But we'd never been able to save much, havin' had eight children in the seventeen years we'd been married, and all of them went with diphtheria except Bobbie. So doctors' bills and funeral expenses kept us in debt; we did the best we could.

"And somehow, when John left me, I went all in a heap, and I was sick a long time, and when I got around again, I didn't seem to have any strength or courage. So when a nice old couple with money offered to adopt Bobbie, and give him the best education money could pay for, I felt that I ought to let him go—I never could have done for him that way.

"He was such a bright little fellow—seven years old, and could read right off in the Bible and the *Old Farmers' Almanac* without stoppin' to spell out hardly a word! Mr. and Mrs. Brown—that was their name—took to him from the start. They had him take their name at the very first. That did hurt somehow, though 'twas right. And kind of them. They'd just bought a fine place over in the next town to Benfield, where I'd always lived, and first I thought I'd see Bobbie often. But they didn't seem to like very well to see me come. What? Oh, no—no! They were very kind, but I guess they thought it kept Bobbie too much stirred up to have Taddy and me droppin' in every little once in a while. I'd a left Taddy with him, but Mrs. Brown didn't like dogs.

"Well, that winter they sold their new place, and

went away, and they fixed it so I never could find out their address—"

"The sthony-hearrted crathurs!" exploded Mrs. Maguire, sitting bolt upright, and dropping Mike's sweater. "Hiv'n'll punish—"

"Oh, no, no, Mrs. Maguire—they thought they were doing the best for Bobbie. They wanted to make a gentleman of him—and so did I. And finally I saw 'twas selfish of me to try to keep a hold on him, when he had such a good chance to grow up different, somehow, and I stopped tryin' to trace him up.

"Well, instead of gainin' strength, I seemed to lose it, after I got to work awhile. I tried to give up the washin' and scrubbin' that I'd tried to do. So when I heard from my husband's cousin Mary—she used to dressmake on this street, but she went back to Benfield for her last sickness—that this little shop was for sale, with the good will and fixtures, and stock, I took the bit of money that was left after the house was sold and the debts paid, and came here to the city and started for myself.

"Hard? Yes, it seemed so, for John had always stood between me and business—still, I'm not the only one that's had to bear hard things. And I've made a livin'.

"But even so, if it hadn't been for Taddy, I don't

know what I'd have done! He was a puppy then, and just as bright for a dog as Bobbie was for a boy. Bobbie taught him a lot of the regular tricks such as other dogs do; but this one he just did was one that Bobbie himself invented. It was intended for an apology, and Taddy was to do it whenever he thought he'd been naughty.

"Well, first after Bobbie went, Taddy'd never do it except when I took him to see Bobbie. But after Bobbie went where we couldn't visit him any more, the little fellow began to do it for me, whenever he saw me lookin' downhearted. The little scalawag had noticed that it made folks laugh, and so he thought 'twould answer that purpose, as well as be an apology. At least, I'm pretty sure that was what was in Taddy's mind.

"But now, for a long time, he hasn't done it. Got out of the way of it when his rheumatism was bad. But this evenin' he saw I was a bit down—this raw weather is so tryin', don't you think?—and that reminded him, bless his heart!

"Haven't I ever heard anything of Bobbie? I was comin' to that. Two years ago an old Benfield neighbor who was sight-seein' here in the city thought she saw Bobbie with a lot of medical students goin' into one of the new buildins of the medical school. She said he looked just as she *knew* Bobbie'd look, grown up. And I thought maybe 'twas here the Browns lived—Benfield's only twenty-five miles out—and it seemed real likely, somehow, that Bobbie'd be learnin' to be a doctor, for he was always doctorin' up sick dogs and cats and birds. I went right out to the school, leavin' Miss Jenks, the neighbor, to tend shop. Seemed as though I couldn't get there soon enough. But no, there wasn't any Robert Brown there studyin'. All the strength went out of me. Not that I meant to thrust myself on him, and mortify him, when he'd got to be a gentleman, but I just thought I could plan to see him once in a while, as he went in and out."

Mrs. Maguire made a noncommittal sound, something between a sob and a grunt. Mary Merivale went on, unheeding.

"No, I'd never thrust myself on him. But somehow, I know it's weak and selfish, but somehow, way down in my heart, I've never give up the idea that sometime Bobbie'd trace *me* out. Mis' Maguire, I've never said this to another livin' bein'. But someway, 'twould seem like Bobbie.

25

"He's twenty-six now, almost. When I go out to close the shop blind at night I can almost *see* him comin' along the street, with his fine, big square shoulders back, and his head up! He looked so much like his father when he was little that I'm almost sure he looks *just* like him now.

"Yes, yes, Mis' Maguire, it is a true sayin'—'If it wa'n't for hope, the heart would break!' Yes, thank God for hope!

"Must you go now? Well, it *is* gettin' late—I've run on so. Yes, I *will* run in soon. Real neighborin' *is* such a comfort. And I can talk freer to you than I ever could to anybody else. You don't try to—to plan for me, or criticize. Just sit and listen, with your face so kind. Rather go in at your back door? Then I'll go out with you to the back gate for a bit of fresh air."

Tad politely preceded the two, as escort. But just outside the gate he caught sight of his ancient foe, the cobbler's big gray cat, and started in ardent pursuit.

"He'll soon be back!" laughed his mistress, and propped the gate ajar with a brick, and left the back door open a bit, as she went about her preparations for the night.

But Tad did not come back, triumphant over a routed

foe, or comically disgruntled over one who had proved far too quick for him.

All night his mistress lay broad awake, getting up every few minutes to go out in the alley and call and listen—but in vain! Morning came at last, and she rose listlessly and opened the little shop, prepared her scanty breakfast, and cleared it away—untouched.

She laid the case before her paper boy, and he enthusiastically enlisted all the neighborhood boys in the search. Heart and soul, and alert eyes and nimble legs, they entered into it, for they were all loyal to Tad and his mistress, and not a boy but was glad to do the little notion shop lady a good turn. Such multitudinously active good will was an unspeakable comfort—but it did not result in Tad.

The first day dragged interminably away, then another, and another. Mary Merivale went out early on that third day to close her blinds. She could not bear to see another customer.

Almost she did not look up and down the street.

"What's the use?" sighed a gray little whisper. But then her brave heart lifted itself once more. She stepped far out on the sidewalk, and raised her eyes.

Round the corner of the street, bright under the last

level sunshine of a perfect December day, a little shape trotted gayly, in front of a stalwart figure—tall, white-clad. Then a succession, no, tangle, of joyous yaps sounded on the still air.

Mary Merivale ran forward a few unsteady steps, and stopped. The athletic figure, seen in the radiant sunlight through her tears, looked like a tall, haloed angel. Strong arms closed around her, and warm kisses rained on her forehead, her lips, her cheeks, her hair!

"Motherdee!"

"Bobbie!"

Suddenly Tad stopped jumping up and trying to climb to their shoulders. They looked down, through joyful tears. There he lay, an appealing paw up, one eye alertly open, and the other screwed tight shut!

"Oh Mother, Mother, 'twas *that* that did it—found you, I mean! Oh Mother, I tried so hard to trace you for a while, after I got to be a big fellow, in high school, and—and sensed things. But I couldn't, for the people who knew where you'd moved, when you gave up the old house, had died, or gone nobody knew where; and all my letters came back. And finally I was told you were dead. And the name and the age in the paper were the same."

"That was your father's cousin Mary. But never mind—now!"

"Oh Mother! And then old Mr. Brown and his wife died suddenly. They'd looked out for me, legally, you know. But the relatives were so—so fresh, that I vowed I'd never take a cent of the money. And I didn't! I'd got a start, and I've worked my way. And I took back my own name, Mother—*our* name!"

"I'm so proud of you; go on, Bobbie boy!"

"Well, I worked my way through college, and medical school, and I'm to graduate this year—this school right here in the city. Mother, think! Here all these years, three years, and never found each other! How can such things be?

"And today, Mother, oh Mother, we—we—Mother, I thought I ought to do it for the good of humanity, but I'll never have part in any such thing again—never! I'll learn some other way! Today we were going to experiment on a dog—yes, a live dog! And everything was ready, and the dog was brought in, and, oh, I'd done such things often enough, and we were joking and laughing. But somehow there was a look in this dog's eyes that—that—well, all of a sudden I wanted to cry; and I felt myself choking up, and I stooped down and patted him—and what did the little chap do but whop over and perform that blessed old trick! Then I remembered—then I *knew*!

"And, Mother, they say medical students get callous—are a hard-hearted lot. But if you could have seen them, and the great surgeon who was to conduct the experiment—we'd had it set late, out of regular hours, to get him—if only you could have seen them, you'd have said their hearts were all right, I can tell you!

"They all came out with me, and Tad struck a beeline for home—*home,* Mother! And I couldn't believe I'd find *you,* but I thought I'd find out *about* you, and where to put the beautiful headstone I meant to buy when I got to earning money, which will be as soon as I graduate, Mother, for a fine old doctor with a big practice is going to take me in with him! And I was hurrying along, when I heard a woman sing out, 'An' sure there's Mary Merivale's dawg—praise the saints!' And then I couldn't come fast enough—and Tad couldn't, either! And then, oh Mother, I saw you standing there, with the sunshine on your dear hair, and the sweet eyes shining, the blessed, beautiful eyes that I remembered so well! And then, oh Mother!"

"Bobbie!"

There was a silence. Then the deep young voice spoke, reverently, as men speak of holy things:

"And it's Christmas Eve, Mother."

The radiant eyes shone up into his.

And Tad? He dutifully began a repetition of his star act, but had his eye only half shut, when he was caught up and carried into the house, his head snuggled down on a broad shoulder, beside a dear, illuminated face, from which he promptly and efficiently licked the queer salty water.

THE STUFFED KITTEN

Mae Hurley Ashworth

J don't know why it is, but oftentimes some of the most memorable stories turn out to be the short-est ones. I know, for I've tried to write short ones, but have never been able to pull it off. I'm convinced that the best ones are divine gifts—they are just given to you.

One of those rare few is this one; and it first came to me many years ago. Like "Christmas in Tin Can Valley," it seemed to me early on that it was too short and too simple to warrant inclusion. But it has been a burr under my saddle every year: in its quiet, gentle, but determined way, nosing itself into my decision-chamber. Since I have been a teacher for over a third of a century, and know whereof Ashworth speaks, I cringe every time I read it. It really says it all.

I have never been able to find anything about the author.

....

ach year at Christmastime, I set out upon the mantel a little old shabby, stuffed toy kitten. It's good for laughs among my friends. They don't know, you see, that the kitten is a kind of memorial—to a child who taught me the true meaning and spirit of living.

The stuffed kitten came into my life when I was quite young, and teaching third grade. It was the day before the Christmas holidays, and at the last recess I was unwrapping the gifts the children had brought me. The day was cold and rainy; so the boys and girls had remained indoors, and they crowded around my desk to watch.

I opened the packages with appropriate exclamations of gratitude over lacy handkerchiefs, pink powder puffs, candy boxes, and other familiar Christmas tributes to teacher.

Finally the last gift had been admired, and the children began drifting away. I started to work on plans for an after-holidays project. When I looked up again, only one child remained at the table looking at the gifts. She did not touch anything. Her arms were stiff at her sides; but her head bent forward a little, so that the thick, jagged locks of her dust-colored hair hung over her eyes.

Poor Agnes, I thought. She looked like a small, dazzled sheepdog.

I had always felt a little guilty about Agnes, because no matter how hard I tried, I couldn't help being annoyed by her. She was neither pretty nor winsome, and her stupidity in class was exhausting.

Most of all, her unrestrained affection offended me. She had a habit of twining her soiled little fingers around my hand, or patting my arm, or fingering my dress. Of course I never actually pushed her away. Dutifully, I endured her love.

"Well, Agnes?" I said now. Abruptly she walked back to her seat, but a moment later I found her beside me again—clutching a toy stuffed kitten.

The kitten's skin was dismal yellow rayon, and its eyes were bright red beads. Agnes thrust it toward me in an agony of emotion. "It's for you," she whispered. "I couldn't buy you anything."

Her face was alive as I had never seen it before. Her eyes, usually dull, were shining. Under the sallowness of her skin spread a faint tinge of pink.

I felt dismayed. Not only did the kitten hold no charms for me, but I sensed that it was Agnes's own new and treasured possession—probably about the only Christmas she'd have.

So I said, "Oh, no, Agnes, you keep it for yourself!"

The shine fled from her eyes, and her shoulders drooped. "You—don't you like this kitten?"

I put on my heartiest manner. "Of course I like it, Agnes. If you are sure you want me to have it, why thank you!"

She set the kitten on its ill-made, wobbly legs atop my desk. And the look on her face—I'll never forget it—was one of abject gratitude.

That afternoon, when the children were preparing to go home, Agnes detached herself from the line at the lockers and came over to my desk. She pushed her moist little hand into mine and whispered, "I'm glad you like the kitten. You *do* like it, don't you?"

I could sense her reaching out for warmth and approval, and I tried to rise to the occasion. "It's quite the nicest desk ornament I've ever had. Now run along, Agnes." I remembered to add, "And have a Merry Christmas."

I watched the children as they marched out and scattered. Agnes started alone down the walk, the rain pelting her bare head.

She was never to return to school. On her way home, a reckless driver ended the small life that had gone almost unnoticed in our community. . . .

....

On Christmas Day, I went to my deserted schoolroom to face the stuffed kitten—and to have it out with my own sick conscience.

Confession is healing, and I felt better after I had poured out my remorse to Agnes's mute gift. The giver was gone, beyond reach of the love and encouragement she had so desperately needed, and that I could have given her.

Or could I have—without Agnes's gift, and without her tragedy. Sometimes the capacity for responding to another's need comes only when the soul is *forced* to expand.

From now on, I promised the stuffed kitten, I would make children my life, not just my living. Besides teaching them the facts found in books. I would look into their hearts with love and with understanding. I'd give them myself, as well as my knowledge.

And heaven help me if I should ever again recoil from a grubby, seeking hand!

GEORGE VON HOESSLIN
MUENCHEN.

SOMETHING QUITE

FORGOTTEN

....

Grace Livingston Hill

*S*ometimes we feel that our age has a monopoly on a flippant attitude toward those who earnestly attempt to make Christ central to their observance of Christmas. This particular story dates back almost three quarters of a century to the Flapper Era, but clearly it could just as well be today the love story portrays.

....

race Livingston Hill (1865–1947) was born in Wellsville, New York, and lived most of her life in Swarthmore, Pennsylvania. A prolific columnist, short story writer, and novelist, she is significant for yet another reason: her works, emphasizing Judeo-Christian values, have remained popular and in print for more than a half century.

....

etty Anderson carefully folded her crisp black velvet dinner dress and laid it without a wrinkle, tissue paper between each fold, into the cardboard box that exactly fitted into her suitcase.

There was a pleased eagerness in her face as she smoothed the velvet across the shoulders, just about the tiny triangle of great-grandmother's bit of old English Honiton lace in the neck. There was absolutely nothing the matter with that dress. It was really distinguished in style, cut, and elegant simplicity.

Betty had always wanted a black velvet dress, but she hadn't thought she could possibly afford it, until she found that wonderful remnant of transparent velvet on the bargain counter, a short-length marked absurdly low. And because she herself was short-length she had been able to get that darling little dinner gown out of the remnant. There had even been enough by careful piecing to make the dear little puffed sleeves that were so short they could hardly be called sleeves at all. But Betty liked a bit of sleeve. She was not the kind of girl who took to low back and slender straps.

She glanced toward the bed, where she assembled the rest of her meager wardrobe, at least all that was respectable to take to the wonderful Christmas house party. Fortunately the party was to be held in a great log cottage up on a mountain, and it was to be supposed that the dressing would not be elaborate in such surroundings, but she could never tell. "Bring sport things and two or three of your prettiest evening frocks," the hostess had said in her casual invitation. So Betty's glance was anxious as she reviewed the collection.

There was a little pool of pink lingerie and the right kind of stockings, quite beyond criticism; black satin slippers with bright buckles, a smart little pair of sports shoes that she had bought for a song because they were too tight for a classmate. Nothing the matter with any of those. It was the dresses that worried her. Had she enough?

There were two hand-knitted dresses which she had made herself in odd hours between studies and when she had to look after the office, for she was working her way through college, and but little of her time was her own. One was brown with vivid orange in the border, the other a lovely Lincoln green with a creamy white blouse with lacy crocheted revera. They were both stylish and distinctive. And, of course, the black velvet was perfect. But besides it she had only two others: The scarlet silk that she had made and dyed herself from an old white china silk of ancient pattern was berry red, Christmasy and becoming. The other was a white satin she had fashioned from her mother's precious wedding dress, high-waisted and quaintly redolent of days long gone.

Well, it was too late to question now. The train left in a little over an hour. She had had to work up to the last minute putting rooms in order before she was free to leave. It was the first Christmas in three years that Betty had spent away from college. Three years since the terrible accident that had swept away Father and Mother and home and fortune in one stroke. It had been a long, hard time, and this was the first bit of change that had come to her. She must not be too particular about whether she had everything that other girls had.

She packed rapidly and gave a quick glance around the room to see if she had left out anything. Ah! There was her Bible. That must go along, of course. She put it in and snapped her suitcase shut. Then she swiftly donned her close green felt hat and lovely new green cloth coat with its beautiful beaver collar and cuffs, rejoicing that some extra coaching she had done in French had made it possible for her to purchase them. Her old hat and coat had been *so* shabby.

She almost missed the train to the city, where she was to meet the party of young people who were to be her fellow guests. Her heart was in a tumult of excitement as she made her way out of the train into the station. But almost at once her ardor was somewhat dampened, for it was a chauffeur in livery who met her at the train gate instead of the bevy of friendly college girls and boys she had pictured.

When she shyly took her place in the middle seat of the third car which the chauffeur assigned her, she most earnestly wished she had never come. "What's the matter, baby? Doesn't your mother know you're out?" cried out a girl with the reddest lips, called "Zaza," for Betty had refused both cigarettes and liquor.

Betty's cheeks flamed crimson and she wanted to cry,

but she knew she must not. They were climbing a hill now, far from any railroad station. It was too late to go back. She must brave it out, and she mustn't let them think her a baby either. She suddenly remembered that she was a witness for the Lord Jesus. She must think of her testimony. A sentence from a book she had read a few days ago came back to her: "The world can only see the Lord Jesus today through men and women who know Him and are willing to slay self and let Him live in them."

Well, she had tried to do that. She had prayed that Christ might be in her all though this Christmastime, even though she might be in a world that did not know Him. But she had not dreamed it would be like this. She would not have chosen to come if she had. Ah! perhaps she had been wrong to be so eager to come . . . to have just the right clothes and everything. Perhaps she had thought more about those things than a child of God should. Well, it was plain now anyway that she must somehow bear a clear testimony among these people while she had to be in their company.

So she endured her discomfort in silence, even taking it sweetly when Rilla Munson, a girl with gorgeous red hair and sharp tongue, carelessly upset her glass on Betty's beautiful new coat sleeve.

That ride was as utterly unlike what she had anticipated as possible. Betty tried to enjoy the woods, the tall forest trees, the plump pines; tried to forget the noisy company about her. Once she even tried to be friendly again, calling attention to a frisky chipmunk in the branches, but Rilla set up a yell to one of the boys: "Oh, Bartley, shoot him for me, that's a darling! I'll have him stuffed for a souvenir!"

The young man actually got out a flashy little revolver and shot several times at the merry little atom of life in the branches. Betty was glad that the yells and screams of the party warned the tiny creature in time and he whisked into a protected hole in a tree trunk, scolding away and looking almost as if he were laughing at them. After that Betty kept her words to herself.

It was early dusk when they arrived at the great palace of logs in the wilderness. It was a wonderful place, with rustic galleries and an immense fireplace filled with burning logs. There were thick rugs and deep soft skins of wild animals on the floor, and great easy chairs and bookcases everywhere, not to mention a grand piano and a number of beautiful works of art not usually found in a wilderness. Betty gazed about in wonder and only wished the company were different. What a wonderful time she could have if they were all nice people!

The hostess was very gracious. She kissed Betty on her cheek, and told the others that Betty's mother had been her schoolmate and she hoped they would show Betty a nice time. But the young people scarcely noticed her and went on about their own concerns.

Betty was given a tiny room at the far end of the upper gallery, only a cot, a dresser, and a chair in it. The hostess apologized, "You won't mind will you, dear? I had to give you this small room because Ted, my son, is bringing home a man he met in Europe and he insists he must have a room to himself."

No, Betty didn't mind. She was only too glad that she didn't have to room with some of those other girls. Having a room to herself, even the tiniest one, might make it possible to endure a good many unpleasant things. She could always get away by herself when things got too hard.

The evening meal was an elaborate and hilarious one. There were twenty young people besides herself, and Betty found it was easy to keep in the background. A few smiles seemed all that was expected of her.

A great deal of the table talk was about the stranger,

Graham Grantland, who was to arrive on the morrow, presumably with Ted, the son of the house. Mrs. Whittington told how brilliant he was and how much Ted adored him, and each girl began clamoring to have him placed beside her at the table. But Zaza declared that he was hers. And then they all began to plan how they would drive up the mountain to meet him on the morrow. Betty took no part in this talk, quietly resolving that she would not be one of those to meet the wonderful expected arrival.

To that end, the next morning she asked her hostess if there was anything she could do to help.

"Oh, my dear, would you?" exclaimed the lady sweetly. "I do want to go down the mountain on an errand, but there hasn't been a thing done about decorations. I wonder if you would look after that for me? You look so sweet yourself I just know you are artistic. The servants will be here to help, of course, and Decker will do all the heavy work. There are plenty of hemlock branches, and holly and mistletoe. Decker will put up the tree. I've told him about that. You'll find the tree ornaments in the attic, and lots of tinsel and tissue paper and silver stars and things. Do you think you could do something to make it look sort of Christmasy here, my dear?"

"Why, I'd love to!" said Betty, her eyes sparkling. "Have you any special plan or directions?"

"Oh, no, dear! Just fix it as you like, make it bright and pretty, that's all. Use anything you find in the house."

With a sigh of relief, Betty turned to watch the noisy guests troop off to the cars and drive away. Then with a zest she went to work.

The three servants took hold with a will. The tree was up in no time, and blossoming out with expensive ornaments and decorations. They chattered like four happy children as they worked. Betty sometimes burst into a Christmas carol and they all joined in timidly, until Betty began to wish it were the servants she was visiting instead of the aristocracy.

All around the second story of the great living room ran a rustic gallery from which opened the guest rooms, and this gallery they interlaced with hemlock boughs. Laurel ropes were festooned from the peak of the lofty roof to the gallery rails till it looked like a tented forest. Holly and mistletoe bloomed out behind antlers on the wall and over doorways. It really was wonderfully pretty. And the giant tree towered and glittered at the upper end of the long room opposite the fireplace.

Everything was done at last but the mantelpiece. Betty looked at it with a catch in her breath; it was a wonderful place to work out an idea. Dared she? Up in the attic she had found a large electric star among the tree trimmings, and a good many rolls of different-colored crepe paper, also a lot of children's toys, among them several large boxes of stone blocks and a whole Noah's ark and zoological garden of animals. These had given her the idea. She called Decker to help her, and with her heart beating a little wildly she set to work.

She made Decker hang up several lengths of deep blue crepe paper reaching from the mantel to the ceiling, and these she peppered over with different sizes of little silver stars which she found in small boxes among the wrappings that had been provided for Christmas gifts.

She feared it was a little temeritous to dare to take down the great deer's head. Crowned with wonderful branching antlers, it had occupied the place over the mantel, but she hung it on the gallery just over the main front door and gave it a lovely collar of holly about its neck. And then she had the electric star hung in the place over the mantel where the deer had been, and framed the whole space in hemlock like a bit of starry sky among the branches.

The servants with growing admiration watched her place a row of little boxes of different heights across the back of the mantel shelf; suddenly, it was not boxes and green paper at all, it was a row of green hills against a midnight sky. Betty was setting little woolly lambs on the hill to the left, with a toy Noah in a brown crepe paper tunic as a shepherd to watch them.

They stood in wonder and watched her deft fingers as she began to build little flat-roofed stone houses from the blocks, with miniature outside staircases on the different heights of the hills to the right. A twig of spruce or hemlock stood here and there for trees. Then all at once a cook exclaimed in wonder, "Sure, that'll be Bethlehem. An' will ye be makin' the stable and a manger?"

So Betty made the inn with little stone arches for entrances, and found three camels with riders for the Wise Men. It was really a lovely picture when it was finished, and it would look quite real when darkness came and all the other lights but the electric star would be turned out.

After a delicious little luncheon by herself, she put on some old togs she found in a closet and went out with a pair of skis to find out if she had lost her old skill acquired several years ago when as a little girl she spent a winter in the mountains.

She was enjoying herself so much that she scarcely noticed how far she had gone until she suddenly began to realize that she was very tried and ought to get back to the house.

But just then she swept around a clump of trees straight into a half-broken trail—and there before her not a stone's throw away stood a horse and a wagon, the horse with his head bent wearily down snuffing the snow, and behind him on the wagon seat two rough-looking men, one drinking from a black bottle, the other reaching to get it for himself.

They both turned as Betty swept into view, an evil light leering from their eyes, and the younger of the two sprang unsteadily down and started toward her. Betty was too frightened to know just what to do, but she gave a quick turn to the right and plunged out through the snow blindly, not noticing until she was actually upon it that there was a deep chasm just ahead that separated her from another rise of the mountain. She caught her breath an instant. She had taken greater leaps than that when a child, but could she do it now? There was no time to think.

"Oh, God, help me!" she cried, and leaped forward, skimming like a bird over the great crack and sailing on down the mountain. When she dared to look back her pursuers were mere specks in the distance. But now what should she do? She dared not retrace her steps to find her footprints back to the house, and she was completely turned around. She had no idea which direction she ought to go.

After a time she came into a quiet place on a higher level and paused to get her bearings. She was surely safe from those awful men! But how was she to get back and be sure not to meet them again? How foolish she had been to come so far. No one would know where to look for her. Somehow she had the impression that the house party wouldn't even notice her absence when they returned, wouldn't bother to hunt for her. Still, of course, someone would eventually make a search. But she mustn't be the cause of all that fuss. She would much rather get back quietly by herself.

Wait! There was a sound! Were those men still on her track? Perhaps they had skis or snowshoes in their wagon. Ah! Was that a shout? The sound drew nearer and she stood listening, alert, but somehow unable to decide which way to move. And then to her great joy the sound grew into words and a voice of gorgeous fullness.

It swept throbbingly among the silence of the trees and snow, like some great organ voice of praise:

"Joy to the world! The Lord is come;
Let earth receive her King,
Let every heart prepare Him room,
And heaven and nature sing!"

Then her heart leaped with relief. Whoever that was, he was singing about her Lord and Saviour, thus she had nothing to fear. The voice was coming closer now, ringing out gloriously with thrilling sweetness and power in the vast mountain silence. It almost seemed as if it must be some great Christmas angel come down from the realms above in answer to her need. Her throat throbbed with longing to join in the song, but she stood waiting, silent, breathless.

Suddenly the singer swept around the mountain and came face-to-face with her! A tall splendid-looking man striding along on skis!

"I beg your pardon," he said, "I supposed I had the mountain to myself. I hope I haven't startled you."

"Oh, I'm so glad you were singing!" cried Betty with

a tremble of tears in her voice. "I've been so frightened by two drunken men that tried to chase me, and when I heard you singing a hymn I knew I need not be afraid."

His face softened and a light came into his eyes. "You know the Lord, too?" he asked, and his voice was almost as if he were claiming kinship.

"Oh, yes!" she breathed shyly.

"That is good. Then we're not strangers. Is there anything that I can do for you?"

"Why, if you could direct me to Strom Castle Mountain, where the Whittingtons live, I shall be grateful. Somehow I'm all turned around."

"Why, that's just where I'm going," said the young man. "Do you happen to be one of the other guests?"

"Oh, yes!" said Betty with relief. "Isn't it a coincidence that I should find you?"

"Well, my name is Graham Grantland. May I know yours?"

"I'm Betty Anderson," she said, giving him a troubled look. "But if you really are Mr. Grantland, how is it that they missed you? They all went down to the station this morning to meet your train. They'll be terribly disappointed."

"They did!" responded the stranger with a grin. "Well, I'm sorry to have made them all that trouble, but I specifically told Ted not to expect me till I got here. I've been visiting friends on a neighboring mountain, and I took a fancy to come on foot and so sent my baggage over by express. However, there's no great harm done, I guess, and I certainly am glad I got here in time to find you, since you were lost."

"I'm afraid," said Betty gravely, "that they're going to be terribly cross at me for having met you first."

"Indeed!" said the young man, studying her keenly. "Well, let them try it!" And suddenly Betty felt deeply thankful that he was here, that she was no longer alone.

"How does it happen that you didn't go down with the rest to meet me?" he asked, a mischievous smile giving him a boyish look.

"Why—I—" Betty hesitated, a bit embarrassed. "I stayed behind to help with the decorations."

"I see," he commented, watching the lovely flushed face and glowing eyes, and reading between her words; "and now, tell me about yourself, please."

As they climbed together to the house on the mountain, the miles flew by on wings. Betty forgot that she had ever been tired. It seemed as if they had known one another a long time. And even though they loitered, they reached the house before the others returned; for, failing to find Grantland on the noon train, they had waited for the late afternoon train to come in. Betty was glad that she did not have to make a spectacular appearance with the lion of the hour. She could just imagine what black looks she would get from the other girls under such circumstances.

But they came a few minutes later, tired and cross and much upset to find that Grantland had arrived during their absence.

Decker, with rare good sense, had turned on only the lights over the front door and in the galleries, so that the full beauty of the decorations would not burst upon the guests until after dinner, for everyone hurried to dress and then rushed down to the dining room.

And so it was that Betty escaped much notice from anyone. She sat at the other end of the table from the guest of honor, beside a disgruntled youth who had been displaced from Zaza's side for Grantland's sake. But occasionally Grantland's understanding glance sought her eyes and she felt somehow that he knew just how out of place she was in this gathering.

58

Finally, in a pause when everybody had been saying how dreadful it was for him to have to walk up the mountainside in all that snow, and how sorry they were that they had not been there to make the afternoon pleasant for him, he raised his voice just the least bit and smiled openly down Betty's way.

"Thank you, that's very kind of you all," he said, "but you needn't apologize. I assure you that I had a wonderful time with Miss Anderson. We were out on skis together for a while. She is a charming substitute hostess, Mrs. Whittington."

"Indeed?" said Mrs. Whittington, turning a cold eye on Betty. "I'm very glad, I'm sure," and a chilling silence fell upon the crowd.

But Grantland still had the ears of the table.

"I don't suppose you knew that our families were old friends," he said, looking at his hostess with a disarming smile. "You see, Miss Anderson's father and my father were close friends and classmates in college, and I was named after Mr. Anderson. Graham Anderson Grantland is my full name. So I am doubly thankful to you for inviting me here, you see."

Betty looked up, a warm thrill running around her heart. So *that* was why he had asked those questions about her dear father; what college he attended and what his exact name was. And then at once the atmosphere about her grew just a trifle warmer. Mrs. Whittington smiled at her and asked her if she had been lonely while they were gone, also remarking that she had noticed there were greens on the galleries and thanked her for attending to the decorations. She hadn't had time to look at them yet, but she was sure they would be very pretty. Even the young man on her left, who hadn't even looked at her before, suddenly grew interested and asked the name of the college she was attending.

With the dessert came a new order of things. The hostess decreed that everyone at the table must tell a story or sing a song or perform some sort of stunt. The hostess picked at random the performers until all had taken part except Betty and Grantland. The others were evidently used to such demands. They had ready the latest joke, the latest jazzy song, and several risqué acts that brought forth wild merriment from the company.

Betty sat with troubled gaze, wondering if she would be called upon, sending up an unspoken prayer for help.

Then her eyes sought Grantland's. What did he think of this? What would he do when they called upon him? The two were the only witnesses for Christ—the Christ who had been forgotten and left out of this Christmas—and what could they do? What would she do if she was called? She couldn't decline, it would not be good sportsmanship or good testimony either.

And even while she was thinking this her hostess called her. "Betty, dear, I'm sure you have some cunning stunt. Give it to us now, please." Betty's frightened eyes glanced down the table, catching Grantland's strong, steady gaze. It seemed to put strength into her and give her courage to follow the idea that had flashed into her mind.

Smiling, she rose to her feet, faced the slightly hostile, astonished company, and spoke in a cool, clear voice: "Would you mind going into the other room for mine? I think everybody has finished dinner, and I need the decorations for a setting. Decker, will you please turn on the lights—*all* the lights, please?"

"Oh, but my dear!" protested the hostess, "everyone hasn't performed. Mr. Grantland hasn't performed, and I imagine his will be the best of all."

"If you don't mind, Mrs. Whittington, I think I too could do better with the setting of the other room," said Grantland courteously, and rose as he spoke.

"Oh, very well," laughed the hostess indulgently, rising and signaling to her guests.

So Betty passed behind their chairs and preceded them into the other room. When the whole company arrived she was standing in her bright scarlet dress beside the fireplace, with the firelight shining on her dark curls. Her eyes were bright with excitement and her face was flushed. As she lifted her eyes and glanced up toward the Bethlehem City she had built, Grantland watched her and thought how lovely she was, and how she might have passed for one of the maidens out of the Old Testament, Ruth or Esther or some Israelite queen in her oriental loveliness. Then, just at that moment, the great star flashed, for Decker had left it till last, and the whole company saw the Bethlehem hills for the first time, and a hush fell upon the room, followed by a soft murmur of astonishment and delight.

Then Betty's voice rose, clear, with arresting attention: "This is Christmas Eve . . ." she said, as if she were calling attention to something they had quite forgotten.

"May I recite the words that belong with this picture on the mantel?" And then, without more preamble, she repeated from memory slowly and distinctly the majestic words of the Christmas Gospel.

As she finished the last words amid a strange, awed silence, Betty suddenly felt frightened at what she had done and shrank back into the shadows.

Then softly into the hush came a tender chord, and another voice, fitting right into the picture as if it had been rehearsed. Grantland had seated himself at the piano and was singing:

> *"O little town of Bethlehem,*
> *How still we see thee lie!*
> *Above thy deep and dreamless sleep*
> *The silent stars go by;*
> *Yet in thy dark streets shineth*
> *The everlasting Light;*
> *The hopes and fears of all the years*
> *Are met in thee to-night."*

The room was very still as the glorious voice rolled on, making the words of the old hymn live anew and forcing their meaning into the hearts of the listeners.

Betty from her shadowed corner looked out in wonder over the hushed company. Over the stairs young Ted Whittington stood, his eyes glowing, watching his friend and drinking in every word. Just below him Dick Atkinson sat on a step with his elbows on his knees, his head in his hands. Everyone in the room looked serious. Even Zaza shaded her eyes with her handkerchief. Back in the open dining room doorway the servants stood in the shadows with bowed heads. Suddenly the tears rushed into Betty's eyes and she had to put her own head down and struggle to keep them back. Ah, the Christ had come back, even to this Christmas! And all those careless people were listening to His story.

On swept the wonderful resonant voice, making a prayer out of the last verse:

> "O Holy child of Bethlehem!
> Descend to us, we pray;
> Cast out our sin and enter in,
> Be born in us to-day.
> We hear the Christmas angels
> The great glad tidings tell;

O come to us, abide with us,
Our Lord Emmanuel!"

There was somehow a holy spell over the rest of that evening. The hilariousness that had ruled at the table did not return. The singer was applauded again and again, and responded with a few more Christmas carols, in some of which they all joined in. Then there was a distribution of the gifts, a rich heap of costly little packages in elaborate wrappings; but even when they laughed there was a subdued undertone in it all.

Zaza did attempt to turn on the Victrola and suggest some dancing, but Rilla shook her head.

"Don't!" she said sharply. "Not tonight! It doesn't belong!"

When at last the company broke up to go to their rest, Grantland sought out Betty in her shadowed corner . . . "How about an hour on the skis in the early morning?" he whispered, "before the others are up."

"Oh, that would be wonderful!" she answered, her eyes like two bright stars.

"All right, then, my new friend, and thank you for the wonderful Christmas story. It was a brave thing to do."

"Oh, but it would have fallen flat if it hadn't been for your singing!" said Betty earnestly.

"Oh, no!" he said quickly, "God's Word never falls flat. Don't you know He has said, 'My word shall not return unto me void, but shall accomplish that whereunto I have sent it?' But I thank God I was here and was allowed to help in the wonderful message your Bethlehem and your story started. Good night, dear new friend! I know I'm going to be thankful always that God brought us together." He pressed her hand quickly, smiled, and was gone.

Betty, full of new joy and wonder, hurried to her little room, to thank her Heavenly Father for the way He had ruled over the evening. But she had scarcely closed her door before there came a tap, and opening it, she found to her dismay that it was Rilla.

"I want to ask you what it is that makes you different from the rest of us," she said when Betty had offered her the only chair and sat down herself upon the cot. "How do you get this way?"

"Why, what way?" asked Betty, puzzled.

"So kind of happy and satisfied-looking," responded Rilla. "You don't seem to have so much to be happy over.

Mrs. Whittington says your people are dead and you've lost your money. I don't see how you can look the way you do. Now, I've got money to burn, and I've tried every thrill in the universe, but I'm just as miserable as I can be. What is it that makes you different? . . . Can you show me how to find it?"

"Oh, yes," said Betty, a great light dawning in her eyes. "It is Jesus Christ! Certainly, I can show you how to find Him."

And there in the little back room, Betty led the way to the manger again, and to the cross, and pointed out the dying Saviour. And presently, with lights turned out, the two girls knelt beside the wide window where the Christmas stars looked down, and Rilla prayed for the first time in her life, accepting the great Christmas gift of a Saviour.

It was long past midnight when Betty at last crept into her cot, a great joy in her heart. Oh, it was wonderful to have had the privilege of leading a soul to Christ!

And in the morning she was to meet her new friend, and she would tell him all about it and he would be glad. Oh, life was wonderful witnessing for the Lord Jesus!

And God had been good to send her a friend like Grantland. A real friend! Oh, this was a glad Christmas Day, indeed!

And she fell asleep thinking of Grantland's good night. Hugging the words to her heart: "Good night, dear new friend, I'm going to be thankful always that God brought us together."

THE STAR IN THE WELL

....

Temple Bailey

ow did the Star get losted?" asked Mary-Alice
*of her mother and father. Since both of them
were responsible—but more so her father—for this loss of
faith, neither knew how to answer her.*

*The answer, and the way back, came during the dark
days of that bleak and cold winter. The answer was not
in the bright feverish city; rather, it was back in the Old
South, a place where values—and the Star—were still*

cherished, a place where love and respect dwelt, whether old or young, black or white.

But it would be in the inky reflections of an ancient well where a father would find his way back and his daughter find her "losted Star."

....

Temple Bailey, author of *"The Locking in of Lisabeth," "And It Was Christmas Morning,"* and *"Candle in the Forest,"* early in this century was one of the most beloved writers in America. Today, a new generation of readers is falling in love with her all over again.

....

Mary-Alice, eating her very soft-boiled egg and her square of buttered toast, was serenely unaware of the stormy forces gathering about the breakfast table until she heard her mother say, with a sob in her voice, "But I hate to think, Michael, that she won't have what we had."

"What did we have?"

"Oh, all the beautiful beliefs about Christmas Day.

And now, we've lost them, you and I—we've lost the shepherds and the angels singing, and the Babe in the Manger, and we've lost the Star."

Mary-Alice reached for another square of toast, but was stopped by her mother's question, "How many have you had, Mary-Alice?"

"Two."

"Drink your milk before you have another."

Mary-Alice having drained her glass, demanded: "How did the Star get losted?"

"There, you see?" said her mother tensely.

"See what?" Michael had risen, and stood looking down at his wife. He was really not thinking of what she was saying; he was admiring the shape of her shining head.

"What can we tell her? Am I to repeat to her what you have just said to me—that Christmas Day is a pagan holdover, that the Wise Men and all the rest are just— poetic fantasies?"

"We must face the truth."

"But what is the truth, Michael?"

And there they were at it again, and Mary-Alice having finished her milk slid down from her chair: " 'Scuse," she murmured, and flitted away, leaving them to their arguments.

She went into the kitchen where Nora Kelly was cleaning out the refrigerator. Nora was on her knees and had set on the floor around her the various dishes which were to be put back on the shelves. There was a part of a cold chicken from the night-before dinner, and a knuckle of ham with plenty of meat on it, and some purple grapes and some pale green ones so icy cold that they had a frosty bloom; and there was a mold of rice for Mary-Alice's lunch, and there was the butter and the bottles of milk, and a jar of French dressing, and lettuce and tomatoes and a square of cream cheese in silver foil, and a mold of Mary-Alice's favorite lemon jelly.

Mary-Alice liked to look at the food on the strong, clean plates. "We've got to give away a lot of it," she told Nora.

Nora turned and stared at her. "Give away what?"

"Things to eat."

"Who'll we give them to?"

"To all the little children who won't have any Christmas."

"Who told you that?" asked Nora Kelly.

"My grandmother."

Nora Kelly waited a moment before she remarked: "I didn't know you had a grandmother."

"Well, I have. Two of them. One of them lives in the country and the other lives with God."

Nora gasped, then went on with her work. After a while she inquired: "Who told you your grandmother lived with God?"

"My other grandmother."

"I'll bet she did," said Nora Kelly. "I'll bet it wasn't your mother or your daddy."

Mary-Alice, being absorbed in watching Nora Kelly fit all the things back into the refrigerator, had felt no further interest in the conversation. She left the kitchen presently to hunt for her doll, and finding her, began to put her to bed, although it was eight o'clock in the morning. Time had little meaning for Mary-Alice. She sang lullabies at any hour of the day, and her lullabies were usually improvised. "The losted Star, the losted Star," she crooned now, monotonously, above the head of the doll.

Her mother, passing through the room and catching the phrase, was troubled. "We shouldn't have talked about it at the breakfast table," she told her husband later. "It is still on Mary-Alice's mind."

"What is on her mind?"

His wife told him, "The things we talked about. We think she isn't listening. But she hears everything. And if she once gets an idea in her head she sticks to it—forever."

It was six weeks before Christmas. Mary-Alice was to have her usual presents. That, her professor-father had decided, was perfectly logical. Gift-giving belonged to the holiday, though one needn't link it up in the least with—superstition.

Mary-Alice wanted another doll, and wrote it on her list. She wanted also a blue doll's crib, a doll's carriage, and a set of dishes.

"But you have so many now," her mother protested.

"Well, we'll have to give all these to the little poor children."

Mary-Alice's father had been pleased when her mother told him. "That's the right spirit," he said, "let us think more of humanity and less of our own souls."

"What about humanity's soul?" Mary-Alice's mother had asked.

"What do you mean?"

"I'd rather give an ideal to a boy or girl than a baby carriage."

Michael laughed, and kissed her. "You'll get away someday from all that."

But Mary wouldn't laugh. "I'd rather come back," she said wistfully, "than get away."

But it wasn't easy for Mary to come back. It was as if everybody in the world agreed with Michael—all the people who wrote books and the people who wrote for the magazines, and the people who talked at dinner parties, and the women in the women's clubs. Mary would put on her trim little suit and the fox fur that Michael had given her, and her dainty and becoming little hat and go and listen to the women while they talked, and it seemed to her that they talked about children's ears and children's eyes, and about having their little minds "psyched" and having their little brains stuffed, and having their little manners mended, and having their tonsils taken out, and having their teeth straightened, but nobody seemed to talk about the children's souls. "Is it because they think they haven't any?" Mary-Alice's mother asked herself. "Yet what would my Mary-Alice be if she were just mind and body?"

She had that, too, to think of when she read the books and magazines. All the heroines of the stories were like leaves blown by the wind, and things happened to them which made Mary-Alice's mother shudder. "I don't want Mary-Alice to be a leaf blown by the wind . . ." and she would shut the books and wonder if there was anyone left in the world who believed in righteousness and faith and the strength of a resolute will.

She talked of these things to Michael. "I can't think of it in the abstract. Mary-Alice is a concrete proposition. We've got to give her a vision. Oh, Michael, don't we know that without vision the people perish?"

But Michael wouldn't listen. "It's all evidence of progress, my darling," he would say. "You must think of that."

"I have thought of it. And I don't get anywhere."

And he would flash a smile at her and refuse to be serious: "I wouldn't bother my brains about it," and after that he would tell her to put on her amber chiffon, or her periwinkle blue, and if she wore the amber he would cry when she came in, "You're all honey-colored, dearest— it is like being with the bees in a field of white clover." And if it was the periwinkle, he would catch her up in his arms and chant, "You are like bluebells . . . blowing in the breeze." And then they would go on to a dance or a faculty dinner. And if it was a dance, Michael would foot it as deftly as a shepherd with his pipe, and the world would seem gay and young. Or if it were a dinner,

Michael would bring all his brilliant brains to bear on the conversation, and would try to prove that we are all puppets pulled by the strings of Fate, and that our efforts to change our lives must end in futility. And Mary would feel that the world was a horrible place, and she wished she didn't have to live in it.

And going home she would wail: "What makes you say such things?"

"Because I believe them."

"You don't really believe them, Michael. It's just that you're puffed up with pride of intellect."

And Michael would laugh triumphantly. "I argued it rather well, didn't I?"

"Too well." For that was the trouble with Michael. He adored blazing trails and breaking down old beliefs, and being called brilliant and broad-minded. So he had thrown overboard everything he had been taught as a child, and he had presented his theories to Mary with such stupendous eloquence that in spite of herself she had been swayed, and now here she was high and dry, and facing what she had to teach Mary-Alice.

And Michael said, "Don't teach her anything. I refuse to let my child be bounded on the right and left by prohibitions. Let her arrive at her beliefs by her own route."

Then Mary challenged him. "She is bounded now by prohibitions. We want her to be strong and well, so we make her eat spinach and drink milk, though we know she hates them. Educationally, she follows our program. We don't let her arrive at learning French without teaching it to her. We don't expect her to be an expert musician without practicing. We tend to her physical needs and her mental needs. We force our theories on her as to diet and to dancing lessons, yet when it comes to matters of the spirit we leave her without guidance."

But Michael wouldn't listen. He lifted her up in his arms. "Go and put on your periwinkle blue," he said, and there it was all over again, with a dinner and a dance, and Michael as gay as a fawn and as splendid as—Lucifer.

It was just a month before Christmas that Michael came home with a cold in his head. He was very hot and feverish and had to be put to bed. After a while the cold went down to his throat and then to his lungs, and he had pneumonia.

And they sent Mary-Alice to the country to be with her grandmother.

Mary-Alice's grandmother was Michael's mother, and she lived in the South, where it wasn't very cold, and she had a great old house with portraits going up and down the stairs, and high beds with carved posts, and high old clocks that ticked and tocked and chimed and struck all at once and everywhere, and a fat silver service was always set before Mary-Alice's grandmother when she poured coffee. In the kitchen there was an aged cook with her head wrapped in a white handkerchief, and her name was Susan and she made waffles and corn cakes and fed them to Mary-Alice surreptitiously, and she stirred up puddings and stuffed chickens, and while she worked she sang strange old tunes in a wailing voice that made little shivers go up and down Mary-Alice's spine. And there were two old hunting dogs who slept on the hall hearth and who thumped their tails when they heard your step, and rose to greet you like gentlemen. And out-of-doors were tall oaks with bare branches, and straight still pines with their rich dark green, and there were borders of box about the old-fashioned garden, and a sundial with ivy leaves twined about it, and in the woods were holly and mistletoe and crow's foot.

There was a fireplace in Mary-Alice's bedroom.

She asked her grandmother, "Why don't we have radiators?"

"My dear child, what would Santa Claus do if he tried to come down the chimney?"

"There isn't any Santa Claus," said Mary-Alice serenely.

Her grandmother, somewhat taken aback, said stoutly, "There's a Christmas spirit."

"There isn't anything," said Mary-Alice. "There isn't any Wise Men or Babe in the Manger, and the Star is losted."

"Who told you that?" her grandmother demanded.

"Daddy."

That night Mary-Alice's grandmother wrote a long letter. In it she told her son Michael what she thought of him. "You are no more learned than your father, Michael, and not half as brilliant. But he used his brains to make men better."

But when she had finished the letter, Mary-Alice's grandmother read it over, and read it again, and then she tore it up and dropped on her knees. "Lord," she said, with her hands folded, "Oh, Lord, he's sick unto death, and I mustn't send it. And show me what to say to Mary-Alice."

But she didn't say anything. She just mothered her in her old arms, and at night before the child went to bed she read to her from a Book, and sometimes Mary-Alice would fall asleep before her grandmother finished, and through the fabric of her dreams the words she had heard would run like a shining thread . . . of still waters and green pastures, and tall white lilies that neither toiled nor spun.

And there came a night when there was a story which was not out of the Book. "It's a legend," Mary-Alice's grandmother told her. "I heard it when I was in the Holy Land. They showed me the Well of the Magi. And they said when the Wise Men were traveling toward Bethlehem with the Star guiding them that the morning light came and the stars were blotted out by the dawning light, even the great Star which they had followed. And the Wise Men wandered on their way, weary and wondering what they should do. And at last they came to a well and stopped to drink. The waters of the well were deep and dark, and as the first Wise Man bent over them he saw mirrored in the deep, dark waters the Star they had lost. And he called to the others and they bent and looked, and behold, there was the Star!"

Mary-Alice, who had been listening sleepily, sat up, wide awake: "But they couldn't see a star in the *daytime*, Grandmother."

"Yes, they could. I've seen stars in our well. Someday I'll show you."

"Tomorrow?"

"Yes. Tomorrow morning."

So the very next day, Mary-Alice went with her grandmother to look into the old well that stood at the edge of the garden. There was a stone wall about it, and a wooden bucket with a chain. The water was sweet and pure, and Mary-Alice reached for the dipper to have a drink.

But her grandmother said: "Before you trouble the waters, look down and you will see the star."

So Mary-Alice looked, and there it was, shining.

And Mary-Alice said, "Then it isn't losted any more?"

"No," said her grandmother, "and it will never be while the world stands."

Now, back in the city at Mary-Alice's home, Michael was fighting for his life. He had two nurses to take care of him, and his wife, Mary, was always in and out. He wanted her all the time, but now and then for her own sake he would send her away. "I mustn't keep you shut up with me, my darling. Go and take a walk and come back with your cheeks rosy."

But with her nights of vigil the roses had gone from Mary's cheeks, and the best she could do when she came in to see Michael was to touch them with color that came out of a little box, so that he might think her gay, while it seemed that her heart was broken.

And when she took her walks, she saw everywhere people buying and buying for Christmas. The windows were full of gifts of all kinds, gifts for Father and gifts for Mother, and gifts for Junior and gifts for Daughter, and toys for the children. People went in a mad rush from counter to counter buying brocade smoking jackets, and diamond brooches, and radios and polo things and skating things.

"They remind me of ants, running about," Mary-Alice's mother said to herself. "What a wonderful thing it would be for the world if all the shops should vanish from our sight, and we should find ourselves crossing a wide plain and kneeling at the threshold of a stable."

And then, in her worry about Michael she would feel that she couldn't be away from him a moment longer, and she would fly back home and beg the nurses to let her sit by her husband's bed.

And sometimes they would let her do it, but at other times they would only let her peep in, and because they had said to Mary over and over again that she must have a bright face and not act as if anything was the matter, Mary would have her hair waved and put on the amber chiffon and the topazes which went so well with it, and Michael, looking at her through fever-burnt eyes, would say hoarsely, "You're all honey-colored, dearest . . . it's like flying with the bees in a field of white clover."

The nurses thought Michael was delirious. But of course he wasn't. He was just a poet. And the next day when she put on the periwinkle blue she knew he would say what he had always said: "You're like bluebells . . . blowing in the breeze."

But when she came in and showed herself, Michael didn't say anything. He was too ill, and the nurses waved Mary away. But she wouldn't go very far. She just stood on the threshold and prayed: "Lord, don't let him leave me . . . don't!"

She didn't know that she was praying. She didn't know that all the things of which Michael had tried to rob her had come back. She only knew that she suddenly found strength to face what might be before her.

That was the day Michael had a dream.

It was a bitter day, when everything outside was all slick and frozen, so that the motor cars slipped and slid over the streets and icicles hung in dangerous daggers at the edges of the roofs, and everyone who had furs was wrapped in them, and those who didn't have them shivered and shook.

But Michael's dream took him away from winter weather, and from the room where the nurses moved in white, and where Mary, his wife, came and stood waveringly in the door, sometimes in a blur of amber and sometimes in a blur of blue, and where he was stabbed with swords of pain, and burnt with irons of fever, and weighted with the tons of heaviness which lay on his chest.

It was spring where Michael went, and in the orchard where he stood the trees were pink and white with bloom and he was a little boy blowing bubbles, and even as he blew them he watched the burnished doves fly down from the roof and wondered what they thought of his bubbles.

Then someone came and sat down beside him. And it was his father. A young father with a thatch of thick gold hair and with shoulders broad under his belted coat, and he said: "It's a wonderful world, isn't it, Michael?"

And Michael said, "Do you like it, Father?"

And his father said, "Yes, don't you?"

And Michael said: "I like blowing bubbles."

And his father laughed and laid a hand on Michael's head: "You don't even know it is a May morning, son, but when you grow up you'll know it."

And after that his father went away. And Michael had forgotten all about it, until now in his dream he remembered the touch of his father's hand on his shoulder. It made him seem so safe in that safe orchard.

The nurses, watching breathlessly, whispered, "He's relaxing a little . . ."

....

I n his dream he found himself now in a great bed. The wind was blowing outside and a storm was coming up . . . the lightning blazed in great sheets across the sky . . . and the thunder boomed. But Michael was not afraid. For his father had come into the room and was speaking. "It's a wonderful storm, Michael . . ."

And Michael climbed down from the bed and stood at the window.

"Do you like it, Father?"

And his father said: "Yes, don't you?"

And Michael said: "If you were not here I should be afraid."

And his father leaned down to him and lifted him in his arms, and they watched the storm until Michael's eyelids had drooped, and he dropped his head on his father's shoulder.

"Look, look," the nurses said, "he is sleeping naturally."

....

And now in his dreams, Michael was an older lad, and he sat in his father's study reading a Book, and as he read his father came in and stood beside him.

And his father said, "It is a wonderful Book, Michael."

And Michael said: "Do you believe it?"

And his father said: "Yes, don't you?"

And Michael said: "If I could only be sure, Father."

And his father laid his hand on his shoulder and said: "Someday you will be sure. You have pride of intellect,

Michael, and you may for a time run with the tide. But my son can never get away from God . . ."

The nurses stared as they looked at Michael in his sleep. "He is smiling."

....

When Mary wrote to Michael's mother, she said: "We are coming up to you for Christmas. The doctor thinks that Michael will be strong enough to travel. We'll get there on Christmas Eve, and, darling mother-of-ours, it will be such a thankful Christmas."

When Michael came he was so thin and white that Susan when she saw him threw her apron over her head and ran back to the kitchen, sobbing. But in a minute she was herself again, and began to give orders about the oyster soup and the chicken jelly which were to be sent up that Michael might refresh himself after his journey, and presently Susan was herself again and was singing the wailing song that had made Mary-Alice shiver.

And Mary-Alice, upstairs on a stool at her father's feet, was telling him about everything.

"An' we found that losted Star, Daddy."

He had to wrench himself back to those ancient days

before his illness. "Oh, yes. . . . Where did you find it, Mary-Alice?"

"In the well. In the daytime. I'll show you."

He said that he had seen it long ago. And after Mary-Alice left, he lay on the couch, looking through the window into the stark gray branches of the big oak. He was all alone in his room, except for the old red setter who remembered him and had stolen in to lie on the rug and lick his hand. It was very different in this quiet room, with its ancestral furnishings, from the bright, bare classrooms at Michael's college. Here were no eager minds challenging him. Nobody to tell him how wonderful he was to have stripped himself free from the past. Here was everything that pertained to the past, to the dignified life built up for him by his father, his grandfather, his great-grandfather, and the men before them . . .

The door opened and Mary came in. She brought on a tray the oyster stew and the chicken jelly. "You should have seen Susan getting it ready. It was a sacred rite."

She set the tray down and drew up a little table. She put a mulberry-patterned bowl on a white cloth and poured the oysters from a hot pitcher. "Everything is as you like it, Michael. And isn't it heaven just to be here?"

He smiled at her and ate his oysters. Not even to

Mary could he express what he was feeling. Yet when he had eaten and drunk, she sat beside him and he held tight to her hand as if he could never let it go.

On the day before Christmas he was up and around but still weak. The house was in a riot of holiday preparation. All the relatives were to come to Christmas dinner and to celebrate Michael's recovery. Mary flying about with tissue paper and seals and red ribbons would stop now and then by Michael's couch to drop a kiss on the top of his head. She came into the living room in the late afternoon to find him in front of the fire, one hand pulling the ears of the red setter thoughtfully, his eyes staring into the coals.

She stood beside him with her hand on his shoulder. "Thinking, Michael?"

He reached up and drew her down to him, crushing her in his arms. "Do you know how wonderful you are?"

"I'm not wonderful, Michael."

"Yes. You are. Mary, at first I loved you for your beauty. But now—if you were gray and toothless—I'd adore you. . . ."

She lay very still in his arms for a little while.

"This old house speaks to me, Mary. Of things I had—forgotten.

"I have thought," he went on haltingly, "as I have sat among his books in his great chair, that I should like to mean to Mary-Alice what my father meant to me. There are things I remember . . . that came to me when I was ill. . . . All through my illness, it was as if my father held my hand . . . and I was not afraid. . . ."

When Mary-Alice awoke on Christmas morning, it was very dark. She did not dare get up, for her mother had told her she must wait until old George came in and lighted the fire.

Old George did not come for a long time. So Mary-Alice lay in bed and was glad it was a featherbed because she sank down into the soft warmth like a nest, and she was aware of her head as very small and round on the big white pillow, and of the wide spaces on each side of her, and of the expanse of counterpane which was really a sun-rising quilt with the sun in yellow calico, only you couldn't see it at this moment because old George hadn't come to make the fire, and you didn't dare get up until he did.

Old George arrived finally, pushing the door open with such caution that Mary-Alice hardly knew he was there until he struck a match and the flames shot up, and she could see her long thin stocking all filled out and fat with things that had been stuffed in it, and Mary-Alice gave a crow of delight at the sight of the stocking, and old George, who was kneeling on the hearth, turned and said in a cautious whisper, "Christmas gif', Miss Ma'y-Alice."

"Merry Christmas, George."

She sat up and talked to him in eager whispers, while the fire burned high and higher, and at last he tore himself away to build the fires in the rooms beyond, and then Mary-Alice crept out of bed. She then found that the old red setter had sneaked in and was sitting by the fire thumping his tail. And Mary-Alice whispered to him. "A Merry Christmas, Rufus," and Rufus thumped his tail harder than ever.

And then all at once Rufus stood up, and Mary-Alice knew that someone was in the room. And she looked around; there was her father. He had on the new dressing gown which Mother had given him. It was blue brocade and his hair was a thatch of gold above it, and there was something in his eyes that Mary-Alice had never seen before. A sort of shining beauty that made them as blue as his gown.

And he sat down in the big chair in front of the fire and took Mary-Alice on his knee, and she showed him her presents and they talked about them, and after a while Michael said:

"Christmas is a wonderful day, isn't?"

And Mary-Alice said, "Do you like it, Daddy?"

And her father said, "Yes, don't you?"

And Mary-Alice said, "Yes. But I thought you didn't."

And before there was time for them to say anything else, Mary-Alice's mother came in, and she said with a catch of her breath, "Michael, you here?"

"Yes, you were sound asleep and I wouldn't wake you."

And Mary-Alice's mother knelt beside the chair and said: "It's almost too beautiful to be true, Michael."

Mary-Alice wasn't sure just what her mother meant by that, but she was sure it must be something which had to do with her daddy's new blue coat and his new blue eyes and that new look in his face which made her love him.

And after breakfast, when they had had the tree and all the presents and Mary-Alice was rocking the new doll to sleep in the new crib, her father came in. He had on a thick coat and carried a cap in his hand, and he said to Mary-Alice, "Will you show me the Star?"

And Mary-Alice sat back on her heels and said: "The one in the well?"

"Yes."

So after Mary-Alice had been buttoned up in her red coat and had pulled her red hat down over her bright curls, they went out together and walked under the bare oak trees and the rich tall pines and along the box hedges and past the sundial, and came at last to the old well; and they leaned over and looked down into the deep dark water.

And there was the Star!

And Mary-Alice's father put his hand on her shoulder and said: "It's a wonderful Star, Mary-Alice. It has shown through all the ages."

And Mary-Alice said: "Mother said it was lost."

"We have found it—together."

And Mary-Alice tucked her hand in her father's hand, and her fingers clung. She had a feeling of great content. She would, she thought, like to hold on tight to her father's hand forever. It was such a strong hand, and she felt—so safe.

TIME TO EXPAND

....

Elsie Singmaster

N o one would ever know! *That's what Charles Keene kept telling himself. And what a difference for himself and his struggling family that money would make.*

And then . . . he looked down and saw a certain look on his little son's face. A look he had known before.

Although this story is well over half a century old, the message is, if anything, even more timely today than when it was written.

*E*lsie Singmaster (1879–1958), born in a Lutheran parsonage at Schuylkill Haven, Pennsylvania, never strayed far from her roots (German on her father's side and English Quaker on her mother's). Her story milieu remained the Pennsylvania German world she knew so well, and its enduring values permeate her writings.

....

*T*ired from traveling over icy mountains, Charles Keene drove his small truck into Carthage at half-past one on Saturday afternoon. A lean, alert little chap with sandy hair and gray eyes, he was the agent of the Phelps Novelty Company, which manufactured iron toys and gadgets.

The December day was dull and the business section of the town dingy. Windows were decorated for Christmas, and ropes of laurel, spangled with electric lightbulbs, festooned the streets. The edges of the laurel were already brown, and the globes, ruby and emerald and glowing topaz at night, were now dull ghosts of those bright shades. Many of the pedestrians were foreigners from the steel mills, and no one who had ever seen the bright attire of their native lands could fail to sigh.

Charles was not depressed by the scene. He was coming home to his family after a week's absence, and he expected to pay a debt today which he had owed for more than a year. He had fifty dollars in his pocket, honestly saved out of his legitimate expense account—this he would give Helen for household expenses; with the hundred and fifty which Dixon Phelps would pay him, he would settle his debt.

He carried his wares in his truck. PHELPS NOVELTY COMPANY was painted on the side and beneath it pictures of toys and gadgets. There was no delay in delivery, which was what the small merchants liked. The Phelps Novelty Company was Dixon Phelps, who had been Charles's classmate in high school. He had a talent for invention, but none for disposing of his inventions. Charles believed that if capital could be found to the amount of even five thousand dollars the business might be started on the way to large profits.

Phelps had only his little foundry, but there was capital in sight. A customer from Pittsburgh had visited him to discuss the possibility of expansion. He looked at

Phelps and his products with respect and at his poor little building with amazement and tried to persuade him to promise not to form a partnership with anyone else.

Phelps was a tall, loose-jointed man, forty years old, with kind brown eyes and graying tousled hair.

"He had great ideas, Charlie," he said. "You couldn't raise any money, could you? I guess he's right—this is the time to expand, if ever."

Charles shook his head. "I have only my house, a little insurance, and a small bank deposit."

"I told him I wouldn't do anything now." Phelps looked away from Charles as he spoke. It was a shame Charles had no money. His father, a lawyer, had left his affairs in lamentable disorder; when his creditors and the old ladies whose money he had pretended to invest were paid, there was not a penny for Charles.

"I have only one debt—that much I can say," said Charles. "We have an old neighbor, Miss Barrows, a retired schoolteacher; when Helen was in the hospital so long, Miss Barrows not only gave her a hundred dollars, but she lent me a hundred and fifty. She told me to leave it until the hospital bills were paid, so she's had quite a wait."

Tired as he was, Charles drove to the plant and made

his report. Probably the customer from Pittsburgh had visited Phelps during the week. If Phelps took a partner, his own position might be jeopardized.

Phelps said nothing about a visitor. His assistant had gone home, work in the factory had ceased for the week, and he sat at the rough desk in his office drawing delicate designs for brackets. He smiled at Charles in his friendly way—Charles was not only his employee, he was his friend and confidant. He took from his pocket a check for a hundred and fifty dollars.

"There's your pay, Charlie."

"The truck's about empty," said Charles. "I've promised delivery of three hundred rabbits early next week."

"Fine!" said Phelps. "They're all ready and many more. The paint'll be dry by Monday morning."

On his way home, Charles made a short detour to avoid passing the Carthage Trust Company. It was in the office of its president, Rowe Hudson, that he had been told the day after his father's funeral that he had nothing. Hudson had been as considerate as possible, but the moment when one learns that one's father has been dishonest is not to be recalled when it can be avoided. Whenever he drove past the Trust Company, he remembered Hudson with his odd little face twisted in concern, the massive furniture in his office, the vitiated air characteristic of banks, and the broad aisle, with the cashier and the teller and the clerks peering through brass grilles.

He put on speed in the last block. Dinner would be over and the two children—Nellie, who was six, and little Charles, who was four—would be taking their naps. Helen was thirty and pretty and capable. Thank God, she was well once more!

He left his truck in the garage at the end of the lot and hurried up the boardwalk, his bag in one hand, a heavy basket in the other. All along his route people knew about Helen and the children; he seldom returned without at least one substantial gift. The basket had been given to him by a merchant in Maytown; the interstices between a jar of apple butter, two pounds of spareribs, and a pan of scrapple were filled with a peck of prize apples.

Helen opened the kitchen door, her eyes shining. "Oh, Charles, I'm so glad to see you!"

Charles set down his basket and bag and took Helen in his arms. He was startled once more by her slenderness, though she had always been slender. If they could only have a woman to do the heaviest work! They could, now that he could pay Miss Barrows. At the thought of Miss Barrows he felt a little sad—when he had paid her, his pocket would be about empty.

"When I'm late it means that I've sold more goods."

"Did you get my letter?"

"I got one, the second day after I left."

"I wrote on Wednesday to say that Miss Barrows died. The funeral was yesterday. I didn't wire because I knew you couldn't come. The Trust Company is her executor and I asked Mr. Hudson whether I might put the house in order. He told me I should find a woman to do the actual work and only superintend it, but I did everything myself. I wanted to. He talked as though there was plenty of money. Do you suppose Miss Barrows was rich?"

"I don't know—not very rich, I guess."

"There are no relatives. I have a feeling, Charles, that she loved you better than anybody in the world."

"She helped me from the time I was a little kid in her school," said Charles. Suddenly the hundred and fifty dollars in his pocket seemed to press against him, as though the check were a sheet of iron instead of paper. His heart leaped. *She did love me,* he thought. *She would never have taken a penny of this money back*. His un-spoken words had a sort of violence, as though he were arguing.

"She didn't really suffer," continued Helen. "It's the way she would have wanted to die. I took her some soup and a tart—and I found her."

"You did, darling?"

"Well, I had the children with me and I told them she was asleep, and got them away quickly. I'm glad you weren't here, you can remember her as she was. . . . The minister spoke beautifully. . . . What did you bring in your basket?"

Charles's heart went thump, thump. *She wouldn't want it back, she'd never take it back!*

"Spareribs and scrapple and apple butter and apples. From the Tanners at Maytown."

"Lovely!" sighed Helen. "Country people little know what it costs to live in the city. I'm going to crochet a purse for Mrs. Tanner. Pork does no harm once in a while. I haven't bought any because it costs so much."

The bank closes at three o'clock, thought Charles. *In any event, I couldn't be expected to see Mr. Hudson this afternoon. I'll surely hear accidentally whether Miss Barrows had more than she needed to bury her.*

If he had not owed Miss Barrows the hundred and fifty dollars, he would certainly have walked around her little brick house with its neat yard and pretty garden; perhaps he would have gone on to the cemetery. Miss Barrows alone spoke to him about his father. The rest of Carthage, even the minister, had observed a silence which they believed to be kind.

"We never know what temptations people have," she said. "Put it behind you! Lift your head! Look 'em in the eye! You've done nothing wrong!"

Miss Barrows was odd; she wore old, old clothes and dressed in bloomers when she worked in her garden. She wrote letters to famous people and received answers— there was no telling what autographs might be found in the confusion of her house. She was always a better gardener than housekeeper.

"I thought I'd let the children sleep as long as they would," said Helen. "Then I'll give them their supper and we'll walk uptown. They turn on the Christmas lights as soon as it's dark. Do you feel like mending some of the ornaments for the tree?"

"I do."

Charles worked at the kitchen table, putting wires into fragile globes and gluing tiny rings. Usually he talked steadily on Saturday afternoons, but today he said little. Helen gave him, now and then, a sidewise glance, praying that nothing had gone wrong. She saw the threatening chasm of poverty even oftener than Charles.

"Well, look here!" cried Charles.

In the doorway stood little Charles. One wrinkled pajama leg was caught up to his knee, his cheeks were scarlet with sleep, his hair curled in wet rings.

"I want to see Daddy," he said.

This house and a little insurance, thought Charles. *And a hundred and fifty dollars.*

Helen swept down upon the baby and gathered him up. "Give Daddy a kiss, then we'll wake Sister. We're going uptown this evening, to see the pretty things. Why, Santa Claus may be walking about!"

Her voice receded as she climbed the steps. Suddenly Charles's face flamed. *We're going to have a few pretty things ourselves,* he determined.

Little Charles walked with him as they went up the street, and Nellie with her mother. Helen had run darts in the back of her six-year-old coat and had relined it; it looked as though it had just come from the shop. The children were always well-dressed at little cost.

Charles's heart felt hard and at the same time light.

The Farmers' and Mechanics' Bank, where he kept his small personal account, was, like the other banks, open from seven till nine on Saturday evenings. What folly it would be to carry his check to Miss Barrows's executors! He would deposit it to his own account; then he would spend part of the cash in his pocket. The children would point out the toys they liked and he would tell the clerks to lay them aside.

The laurel looked green and velvety, the bulbs shone like emeralds and rubies and topazes. Every window was decorated; here a stable was set in an Oriental landscape, here another was half hidden by evergreens. Santa Claus shouldered his way along, giving candy to children. Nellie and little Charles laughed at the tops of their voices. Their gaiety disturbed Charles. *I'm tired*, he thought. *Tired and irritable.*

Dixon Phelps stood looking into the central square, his shoulders bent, his hands deep in his coat pockets. Charles had intended to go up the street to the Farmers' and Mechanics' Bank, but both children ran to join Phelps. This did not change his purpose to deposit the check to his own account. He would leave Helen and the children with Phelps and rejoin them. Little Charles put one warm hand back in his father's.

"Hello!" said Phelps. "I told a man up here in a store that I was going to bring a young lady and gentleman to see him."

"You'll surely be on hand Christmas Day, Dixon," said Helen.

"I surely will! I used to stand here on Saturday evenings with my father—on this very spot. No matter how tired he was, he always brought me to town to have ice cream. I'll never lose the habit, I guess."

Charles answered without meaning to answer. He never spoke of his father, or thought of him when he could help it. Now thought and speech were involuntary, like a sudden spurt of water from a dammed-up flood. He saw himself standing on this very spot, his hand held tight.

"My father did the same thing. I remember—" He did not say what he remembered.

The eyes of Helen and Phelps met swiftly, and as swiftly parted. Helen felt an impulse to put her hand on Charles's arm, but she resisted. "Here comes Santa!" she cried.

"There are few fathers who don't mean to do their best by their children," said Phelps.

Little Charles tried to pull his father and Phelps with

him to meet Santa Claus. Charles did not feel the tug of the little hand or see Santa Claus. Instead, he saw, under gaslights dim as the moon compared with these lights, himself and his father coming hand in hand down the street. He could have expressed his thought to Miss Barrows, but to no one else, not even to Helen. *He made mistakes, but he loved me.* He looked down at little Charles; he could not tell for an instant whether this was little Charles looking up at him, or whether he stood there looking up at his father. Both looks adored. *But love isn't enough!* he decided.

"Come, Daddy!" begged little Charles.

Charles pulled his hand away, almost roughly. "I'll find you," he promised.

He walked past the turn which led to the Farmers' and Mechanics' Bank and around the square to the Trust Company. There was a tree on each side of the step. He had not entered the door for ten years; he was amazed once more at the height of the ceiling, supported by gilded beams. It was the bank of the steel works, and there were a hundred patrons waiting their turns at the windows or sitting on the settees. A woman was smilingly receiving Christmas savings—the face of Santa Claus was printed on the check. Charles had often wished to make a deposit each week and have it swell to a sizable sum by December, but he could never spare enough to make the deposits.

He walked down the aisle toward Mr. Hudson's office. A clerk was typing in the anteroom; the office itself was behind a mahogany door. The clerk asked him to wait and he sat on the edge of a chair. What a shamed, confused half-hour he had spent on the other side of that closed door!

My youth ended there, he sighed wearily.

Hudson sat behind his desk when at last Charles was admitted. He was not only odd-looking, he was an odd sort of man for a banker. He handled money as though it were only paper and metal; his joy was in his Bible class and his garden. When he saw Charles, his eyes narrowed and he began to moisten his lips with his tongue. He caught his lower lip between his teeth and let it go and caught it again—Charles remembered each mannerism. On his face was the strange, exalted expression which his Bible class saw before he started to pray.

"Sit down, Charles," he said. "Glad to see you."

Charles continued to stand while he took Phelps's check from his breast pocket. "I learned when I came home this afternoon that Miss Barrows had died."

"Yes," said Hudson. "She was a good woman."

"She was a good friend," said Charles. "She gave my wife a present of a hundred dollars when she was sick. When things got very bad, I borrowed a hundred and fifty from her. She didn't wish a note, and she refused interest. . . . She said not to bother until the hospital bills were paid. It took a long time. Today, I wish to pay the money to her estate."

He took out his fountain pen and leaned over the desk. "Pay to the estate of Caroline Barrows," he wrote, and signed his name and handed the check to Hudson.

Hudson continued to chew his lip. A minute passed . . . another. It seemed to Charles that Hudson was making an effort to tell him something—to break something to him. His heart filled with dread. The hundred dollars was a gift, they couldn't ask for that back! Or was there something else, something about his father, cropping up? He did not realize that he lifted both hands to his head.

"Please sit down," insisted Hudson. "I want to talk to you."

"I left Mrs. Keene on the street corner with the children."

"I don't wish to alarm you," said Hudson. "There's

nothing to alarm. Find Mrs. Keene and tell her you'll join her directly, if that will make you more comfortable."

Charles stepped into the outer office, past the typist and through the low gate. He saw, entering the far door, Helen and Phelps, Phelps with a child attached to each hand. He went to meet them.

"We came to find you," said Helen.

"Mr. Hudson wishes to talk to me," explained Charles. "I don't suppose he'll want me long."

Once more the glances of Helen and Phelps met. *Oh, what has happened to him?* cried one glance to the other.

Phelps drew the children to one of the benches. "Let's watch the people. Perhaps Santa'll come in here."

Helen slipped her hand in Charles's arm. "Will Mr. Hudson object to seeing me, too?"

The typist opened Hudson's door, and Charles and Helen went in. The vice-president of the bank, Orton Harlow, taller, larger, handsomer, and much more loquacious than Hudson, stood beside Hudson's desk. He was a man of the world, a bachelor who found his pleasure in golf and visits to New York. He noted Helen's dark eyes and her wavy hair and her slender figure.

"Hello, Charles!" he said genially, though he was

scarcely acquainted with Charles. "Mrs. Keene, good evening!"

"I came to look for my husband," said Helen.

Harlow pushed forward a chair. "With your husband is where you belong at this moment."

"Sit down, Charles," invited Hudson for the third time.

Charles sat in a heavy chair beside the desk. Here in this very spot he had sat ten years ago. His arms shook, he heard Hudson speaking, but he did not take in what he said. Hudson had three sheets of heavy foolscap before him. One lay open, the others were folded, wrapped with cord and sealed with sealing-wax. One had a large and distinct #1 written on it, the other #2.

Hudson lifted the open paper and spread it before Charles. On it were a dozen lines of writing. Hudson bit his lower lip; he was half-frowning, half-smiling.

"Miss Barrows had her own ideas," said he.

Charles did not hold the paper; he turned the heavy chair so that he might rest his elbows on the desk and look down upon it.

"I direct my executors, the Carthage Trust Company, to pay my funeral expenses and provide for me a simple tombstone," he read. "My young friend, Charles

Keene, to whom I have been attached since his boyhood, is indebted to me to the sum of one hundred and fifty dollars. If he pays this sum to my executors within a month after my death, or reports that he owes it, my executors are to probate that will of my two wills which is marked #1. I believe that Charles will do this. In this case, Will #2 is to be destroyed unopened.

"In case he does not, within a month after my death, pay the sum of one hundred and fifty dollars to my executors or report to them that he owes me this sum, my Will #2 is to be probated and my Will #1 is to be destroyed unopened."

Hudson lifted the paper and passed it to Helen. "I can't read it!" cried Helen, her face stricken.

Hudson took it back and read it aloud.

"Did you owe her a hundred and fifty dollars?" asked Helen, clearly fearing his answer.

Hudson lifted Phelps's check. "He came in this evening to pay it." He laid down the check and lifted Will #1, so plainly marked and so elaborately sealed, and slit the string and broke open the seals. Harlow read the writing with him, looking over his shoulder.

"Here!" cried Hudson, and spread the will out before Charles. He leaned over the desk and held it flat for

Charles to see. Charles propped his head on his hands and read. Then he lowered his head to his folded arms.

Helen started to rise, but she sank back, trembling. Harlow lifted the paper and came round the desk and held it under her eyes. "My hand shakes!" he said with a laugh. "This you can surely read, Mrs. Keene!"

There were two lines, like the other writing in a legible schoolteacher script—Helen read them three times before she understood what they said.

"My estate is to become the property of my single and only heir, Charles Keene."

"You don't even ask what Caroline Barrows had!" said Harlow after a long time. "Well, that which remains is somewhere around twelve thousand dollars."[1]

[1] Around $250,000 in today's money.

HOLDING THE PAN GINGERLY AND
STIRRING THE BUBBLING GRAVY

THE RED ENVELOPE

....

Nancy N. Rue

om was gone. How could she possibly face Christmas without him? Worse yet, the children were all acting as if it was Christmas as usual. How could *they!*

....

ancy Rue, of Lebanon, Tennessee, is a frequent contributor to Brio *and* Breakaway *magazines.*

She is also author of the Christian Heritage historical fiction series published by Focus on the Family. "The Red Envelope" was the lead story in the December 1997 Focus on the Family Magazine.

....

Slice.Scoop.Plop.
I don't feel like doing this.
Slice.Scoop.Plop.
I don't want to do this. I don't want to shop—
Slice.Scoop.Plop.
I don't want to decorate. I just want to skip it—
Slice.Scoop.Plop.
And pretend I didn't notice this year.

J sliced, scooped, and plopped the last of the dough from the ready-made cookie dough package and shoved the cookie sheet into the oven. They were a far cry from the bejeweled affairs I'd baked for twenty-six years, and the only reason I'd even summoned up the effort to throw these on a pan was because Ben had opened and reopened the cookie jar four times the previous night before saying with fourteen-year-old tact, "What—you're not baking this year? What's up with that?"

He'd gone on to inform me that tomorrow—now today—*was* the twenty-third and that Ginger and Paul would be arriving in two days, and they were going to "freak" when there wasn't any "cool stuff to eat, like usual." This from the same kid who flipped the channel every time a holiday commercial came on and had for years been eschewing all talk of a family photo for the annual Christmas card.

I hadn't even considered a family picture this year. A big piece of the family was now missing—or hadn't anybody noticed?

All my friends had been telling me practically since the day of the funeral, "Michelle, the first year after you lose your husband is the hardest. You have to go through the first Valentine's Day without him, the first birthday, the first anniversary—"

They hadn't been kidding. What they hadn't told me was that Christmas was going to surpass all of them in hard-to-take. It wasn't that Ken had loved Christmas that much. He was as bad as Ben and Scrooge put together when it came to holiday advertisements—said the whole thing was too commercial and that when you really thought about it, Easter was a much more important celebration in the church.

I flopped down on a stool at the kitchen counter and halfheartedly started a list of who I needed to buy for. Ginger had called last night—right after Ben's fifth trip to the empty cookie receptacle—giggling and shushing the dormitory howls behind her.

"I just finished my last final!" she shrieked into the phone. "I'll be home day after tomorrow. Do you know what I'm looking forward to?"

"Sleeping for seventy-two straight hours?" I said.

"No." She'd sounded a little deflated. "Seeing all those presents piled up under the tree. I've never cared what was in them or how many were for me—I just like seeing them there. How weird is that?"

Not weird at all, my love, I thought now as I penciled in Ben, Ginger, Paul, his wife Amy, my grandson Danny. *Just highly unlikely.*

I hadn't done any shopping. I couldn't even think about my tradition of wrapping every gift so that it was more a work of art on the outside than the article within. And there had been no way I could spend my usual three days decorating—two hours on the manger scene alone.

But my kids were still expecting it—even Paul, who at twenty-five had a child of his own and *still* asked me last week when he called if I had the old *John Denver Christmas* album dusted off yet.

I snapped the pencil down on the counter. None of them seemed to even suspect that this wasn't going to be the usual Tabb family Christmas. They were all acting as if their father's death eleven months ago wasn't going to change a thing about our celebration. As far as I was concerned, there wasn't that much to deck the halls about. Ken was gone. I was empty and unmotivated and at best annoyed. At worst, I wished they'd all just open the presents and carve the turkey without me.

When the oven dinged, I piled two dozen plain brown circles on a plate and left a note for Ben: I DON'T WANT TO HEAR ANY MORE COMPLAINING! GONE SHOPPING. I LOVE YOU. MOM.

The complaining, however, went on in my head as I elbowed my way through the mob at the mall.

Ken was right, I thought. *This is all a joke.*

It really was everything he hated—canned music droning its false merriment somewhere in the nebulous background—garish signs luring me to buy—squabbling, tired-looking families dragging themselves around, worrying about their credit card limits as they snapped at their children.

Funny, I thought while gazing sightlessly at a display of earrings I knew neither Ginger nor Amy would wear, *all the time Ken was here pointing all this out to me, it never bothered me. Now it's all I can see.*

I abandoned the earring idea and took to wandering the mall, hoping for inspiration so Ginger would have something to look at under the tree. It wasn't going to be like years past—I should have told her that. She wasn't going to see the knee-deep collection of exquisitely wrapped treasures that Ken always shook his head over while he grinned at me.

"You've gone hog-wild again," he would always tell me, and then he would add his one contribution. Every year he spent months looking for just the right worthy cause. Instead of buying me a gift, he'd write a check in my name to them—be it the Muscular Dystrophy Association or a local church that needed a new roof— and put it in a red envelope and tuck it onto a branch of our Christmas tree.

"This'll last all year," he'd tell me. "Maybe even change someone's life."

I stopped in mid-mall, causing a pileup of aggravated shoppers behind me.

Ken wasn't there, a fact that didn't seem to bother the rest of my family. But he could still be with me, maybe just a little, if his part of Christmas was.

It wasn't a big spark of Christmas spirit—but it was enough to ram me through Sears and Wal-Mart—and See's candies. Paul liked the cashew turtles. It was also enough to nudge me with the fact that I couldn't put the envelope on the tree if we didn't have a tree. They still had some left at Safeway—and their turkeys looked good, too.

The decorations weren't buried too deeply in the garage. I'd barely gotten them put away last year before Ken had his heart attack. I thought about that as I dragged in boxes and untangled lights. The American Heart Association—that was the ticket. I stopped and wrote a check and miraculously located a red envelope in my desk. It would look perfect on this branch—what else to put there—I didn't get candy canes for the tree this year—maybe I'd string some popcorn—

I was deep into decorating when Ben emerged from the kitchen.

"Where are the rest of the cookies?" he said.

"What do you mean, 'the rest'?" I said. "There are two dozen on that plate."

"Were," Ben said.

I rolled my eyes at him as I backed up to check out the tree. "I'll make some more," I said.

"Are you going to put thingies on the next batch?" he said.

When I finished setting up the manger scene, I checked the kitchen for "thingies."

But the next day—Christmas Eve—my spirits sagged again. There is no lonelier feeling than standing in the midst of one's family—squealing, vivacious college daughter; sweet, gentle daughter-in-law; handsome, successful quarter-century son; wide-eyed, supercharged four-year-old grandson; and even an awkward teenager whose hugs are like wet shoelaces—and being keenly aware that someone is missing.

Everyone else seemed to be avoiding the subject.

"The tree is *gorgeous*, Mom," Ginger said. She knelt in front of it and began hauling gifts out of a shopping bag to add to my pile.

"I love what you did with the wrappings, Michelle," Amy said. "You're always so creative."

"I forgot to buy wrapping paper," I told her. "I *had* to use newspaper."

None of *them* had forgotten a thing. There was no sign of mourning—it was Christmas as usual. Ben and Paul sparred over whose stocking was whose and Danny picked all the M&M's out of the cookies before he ate them and Ginger picked up every present and shook it. I put on a valiant smile and wished they would all go to bed so we could get this over with.

I stayed up after the last of them and slid my red envelope out from under my desk blotter. The tree lights winked softly at me as I tucked it between a misshapen glittery angel Ginger had made in second grade and Ben's Baby's First Christmas ball.

"I guess they have to go on with their lives, Ken," I whispered. "But I wish you were here."

It occurred to me as I unplugged the lights and groped toward the stairs that they might feel a little ashamed in the morning when they realized what it was. Would there be some, "Oh, yeah—I remember he always did that—" and some gulping and some exchanging of sheepish looks?

I hoped so.

Danny was, of course, up before the paper carrier. I dragged myself into the kitchen and found it already smelling like a Seattle coffee house.

"This is what we drink at school," Ginger told me, and handed me a cup.

"Have they already started on the presents?" I said.

She shook her heard, and for the first time I noticed a twinkle in her eye that was unprecedented for this hour of the morning.

"What are you up to?" I said.

"It's not just me," she said.

"Mom!" Paul yelled from that direction. "Come on—I can only hold this kid off for so long!"

"Come see'm, Gramma!" Danny called. "Come see all these red things!"

"What's he talking about?" I said.

"You'll see," Ginger said.

What I saw at first was my family, perched on the couch like a row of deliciously guilty canaries. What I saw next was our Christmas tree, dotted with bright red envelopes.

"Man, it got crowded in here last night," Ben said. "I came down here about two o'clock and freaked Amy out."

"I almost called 911 when I came down," Paul said. "Till I saw it was Ginger and not some burglar."

I missed most of that. I was standing in front of the tree, touching each one of the five envelopes I hadn't put there.

"Open them, Mom," Ginger said. "This was always the best part of Christmas."

Paul chuckled. "I was afraid everybody had forgotten."

No one had. From Paul, there was a check for Big Brothers, for kids who have to grow up without dads. From Amy, to the church, where she best remembered her father-in-law. From Ginger, for the Committee to Aid Abused Women—"because Dad always treated you like a queen," she said. From Ben, a twenty-dollar bill for a local drug program for kids, "since Dad was all freaked out about me staying clean."

The last envelope was lumpy and it jingled. When I opened it a handful of change tumbled out.

"That's from me, Gramma," Danny said, little bow-mouth pursed importantly. "For lost dogs—you know, like that one me an' Grandpa rescued."

I shot Paul a question with my eyes.

"He brought it up himself," Paul said.

Amy groaned happily. "He remembered at five o'clock this morning."

I pulled all the envelopes against my chest and hugged them.

"You know what's weird?" Ginger said. "I feel like Daddy's right here with us."

"Yeah, that's pretty weird," Ben said.

"But true," Paul said. "I felt like he's been here this whole time. I thought I'd be all bummed out this Christmas—but I don't need to be."

"Well, Ken," Amy said. She held up her coffee mug. "Here's to you."

Mugs clinked. Laughter danced across the living room.

I began to think about carving that turkey.

JOE WHEELER, Ph.D., Emeritus Professor of English at Columbia Union College in Maryland, compiled the four volumes in the *Christmas in My Heart*® series. He is Senior Fellow for Cultural Studies at the Center for the New West in Denver. He has established nine libraries in schools and colleges and continues work on his own collection (as large as some college libraries). Joe and his wife, Connie, are the parents of two grown children, Greg and Michelle, and make their home in Conifer, Colorado.